CW01211271

The Birth Mother

AJ Carter

Papyrus
PUBLISHING

contact@ajcarterbooks.com

Dedication

For my daughter, who inspires everything I do.

And for my dog, who farts in her sleep.

The Birth Mother

by AJ Carter

Prologue

LET me tell you about how my daughter went missing.

I'll spare you the superfluous details – the usual waste of words about letting out breaths I didn't know I'd been holding or even throwing my unwashed hair into a ponytail. This isn't about exhalation or hairstyles at all.

It's about the monster who came to stay.

And everything she took from me.

Chapter 1
Lizzie

THE HORN MAKES me jump out of my skin, instantly yanking me from my exhausted daydream. My hand shoots up in apology while I spin the wheel and pull the car over to the side of the road. The driver behind – a woman I recognise from previous school pickups – gives a scolding glare as she drives past. Normally, that might bother me.

But I'm just excited to see my little girl.

She comes in like a hurricane. 'Hurricane Amy' is what we call her. She's everything you can expect from a blonde-haired, blue-eyed five-year-old with a cheeky grin and buckets of energy. The car immediately lights up with joy as she climbs into the back seat, clips in her seat belt, and pulls the door shut.

'Ready?' I ask, waiting for the signal.

'Go!' Amy screams, giggling as if she's just robbed a bank and I'm her getaway driver.

Unfortunately, we don't get very far. The traffic has built up ahead of us, taking up the whole narrow street. The woman who passed me a minute ago is leaning on her horn again, as if expecting everyone to turn on the *FLY* function on their cars and DeLorean their way out of there. It's a dead effort. She's as stuck as the rest of us.

'The police are coming for us!' Amy yells with a smile. I watch her in the mirror, leaning against the restraint of her seat belt while she tries to peer over the back seat and through the rear window. 'Step on it, buddy!'

I can't help but laugh. Although it's a mystery as to where she got the idea for this little game, it's still endearing and fun. As always, she manages to make me ignore my fatigue and join in. Playing with my little girl is the best part of any day.

'We're stuck in the mud,' I yell back. 'Looks like we're going to jail!'

'Oh, no!'

Suddenly, we both burst into a fit of laughter.

Amy's high-pitched chuckle makes her sound like a chipmunk, and my eyes are watering from both laughter and intense love. I always wanted to have a kid, and no matter how hard things sometimes get, it's the best thing ever.

Amy pulls the notebook out of her backpack and starts drafting an escape plan. Meanwhile, the traffic starts to move, albeit slowly. I lift off the clutch, and we roll forward just a few more feet. Amy slinks back in her seat, blowing out a breath as if her school day has just caught up with her. It reminds me of how badly I need to lie down for a bit.

As if that's an option.

The next time a car inches forward, movement catches my eye. I turn my head as an instant reaction, expecting to see someone in the parked car beside me. What I quickly realise is that nobody is *inside* the car, but an eerie figure is standing on the opposite side of it.

And they're staring right at us.

My entire body floods with cold. I look away, shivering with discomfort, then turn back to look again. This time, the figure is gone from the window, disappearing into the flood of parents who are picking up their kids. When another car honks behind me, I'm torn out of the moment and forced onward through the slow crawl of traffic.

Did I imagine that, I wonder? Was there really someone watching us, or are the late nights and early mornings finally taking their toll on me? Whether or not it was my imagination, there's one thing about the last few seconds that's undeniable.

I feel vulnerable... and instantly defensive.

As is sometimes the case, there's nowhere to park on our own street. The closest spot I can find is halfway down the road, where I perform the best parallel parking of my entire life as a bead of sweat drips down my temple. It doesn't bother me – the cold October weather will soon bring the chill back.

'Good job, Mummy,' Amy cheers from the back seat.

'Thanks, Little Goof.'

'Yuk. I hate it when you call me that.'

'Do you know *why* we call you it?'

'Because I'm little.'

'That's right. And?'

'Because I'm goofy.'

'Yes.' I nod approvingly, meeting her proud

gaze in the rear-view mirror. 'Approximately one hundred per cent of the time. Now, get your bag and let's go.'

Amy laughs once again as she opens the door and springs out. I follow in her overly excited footsteps, locking the car and trudging behind her all the way to the house. She's only a few feet ahead, but I ask her to hang back a little. Amy's a good kid, and she usually listens, but this time, she runs ahead as if it's some kind of race.

She doesn't stop until she sees *him*.

I stop, too, quickly assessing my options. Ed is a lovely man who's lived next door to us for years. Here's everything I know about him: he's lived in Longwell Green for most of his life with the woman he married in the 1950s; she died of cancer ten years ago, and now he's very lonely; he's a busybody; he likes to travel but refuses to do it alone, which means he doesn't go anywhere; he's a busybody; everybody avoids talking to him because his conversations never end. Also, in case I didn't mention it before... he's a busybody.

'Location obstructed. Over,' Amy says into her palm as if it's a radio. She always wanted to be a police officer, but it's one of the many dream jobs she constantly cycles through. It's likely to be a nurse or a pop star next week.

I raise my hand and mouth into it, 'Acknowledged. Suggest alternative path. Over.'

'Negative. Engaging target.'

Amy runs on before I can stop her, fanning her hands around to catch Ed's attention. It doesn't take long for him to spot her – it seems all he was doing was walking up and down the street anyway, so now that he's found somebody to talk to, the damage is as good as done.

I catch up to where they're standing, effectively blocking the path to my own front door. Sometimes I wish my husband wouldn't work away from home for so long. He's excellent at getting rid of Ed. Or, at the very least, taking the heat so I can get inside and start the dinner.

'Are you ready for Halloween?' Ed asks, mostly to Amy.

'Not quite,' I intercept. 'Plenty of decorations to go up and not enough time.'

'It never was my favourite time of year. All those ghosts and goblins and things that go bump in the night.' Ed waves his fingers like writhing worms and pulls a face at Amy, who giggles politely. He turns from her, then raises his dusty eyebrows up the street. 'Where did you have to park today?'

'Just up the road.'

'It's not right, you know. I should talk to the council about this.'

'If you must.' I smile softly and try to squeeze past, encouraging Amy as I go. She snatches the keys from my hand, slides through the gap easily, then says goodbye to Ed. As soon as she's through the front door, I use her as an excuse to follow suit. 'I should—'

'Now that she's gone...' Ed leans in and lowers his voice. 'Have you seen her?'

'Who?'

'The woman.'

'What woman?'

'That was precisely to be my next question.' He raises a liver-spotted hand to brush some thinning, grey hair away from his face. The autumn wind stubbornly brushes it back within two seconds. 'I've seen her a lot lately, walking up and down the street, slowing down every time she passes your house. I didn't want to mention it in front of Amy because it might scare her, but you ought to be careful. It looked very suspicious.'

Naturally, the news hits me like a brick

tumbling out of the sky. My mind flits back to the trip home from school, where I was almost certain someone had been glaring at me through a car window. Are they the same person, or am I putting two and two together to get five?

'I'd better go in and make sure Amy is okay,' I tell him.

Before he can try to stop me, I turn on my heel and march into the house, quickly closing the door my daughter had left open for me. It's only in the last couple of seconds that I hear Ed's final words. Then, for the second time today, my entire body turns to ice.

'Be careful,' he says. 'Something's wrong.'

As you can expect, I did all I could to put that thought out of my head. Sure, I had to remain wary in case some strange lady came knocking on my door in the dead of night, but it didn't come to that. All I had was a long, sleepless night as the house creaked and groaned in the rising winds. You might say I was paranoid.

On the bright side, I've woken up to a clean, tidy house. Amy got up before me and sorted out her own breakfast. She's good at it, just like she is with everything, but I never want her to feel like her own mother won't take care of her. If she ever needs anything, all she has to do is ask. And maybe poke me a little if I'm sleeping.

Coffee mug in hand, I do a short walk of the large, well-furnished house while keeping an eye out for anything she might need in her school backpack. It's not too difficult – although our house is big and a lot to manage, I somehow get by. It's easier when Chris is home, but God knows when the next time will be. He drives across the country for a living. Not that we need the money, but he enjoys his independence and the freedom of the road, even if it is for weeks at a time. You probably think that sounds like a nightmare, but we do both enjoy our private time. Besides, absence makes the heart grow fonder, right?

By the time I get Amy out of the door and into the car, I've almost completely forgotten about Ed's report. It's the final day of school, and I've got a whole day of chores to do before the world's best five-year-old keeps me on my toes for over a week.

'Mother,' she says as we begin our short commute.

'Daughter,' I respond.

'What are we going to do during school holidays?'

'Anything you want. Within reason. Did you have something in mind?'

'No, but I'll get back to you in due course.'

A smile parts my lips as I focus on driving. I really have no idea where she gets these little expressions, but I'm guessing it's from TV or over-hearing teachers talking near the playground. The thought continues to amuse me for the rest of the journey, and we're there before we know it. The school rush is over, and we're right on time.

Thanking my lucky stars that I managed to get a parking space, I hop out and walk Amy to the gates. We kiss goodbye as always, and I return to the car with the same gaping hole in my stomach that always comes with leaving my daughter.

But that feeling is soon replaced by dread.

The figure has returned to the street, but it's clearer this time. With only a small car to stand behind, it's easy to see the raggedy red hair blowing around in the whistling wind. The moth-eaten, hippie-looking clothes are colourful but faded, and they hang off her like curtains. If I'd encountered her in the dark, I'd be way too scared to approach.

But with the safety of school security right behind me, I waste no time in marching across the street.

'Hey,' I call out, snapping my fingers to break her stare.

The woman – definitely a woman and more than likely the same one Ed is concerned about – stands up straight and hurries away. I stumble to catch up, but a car stops right in my way. My breath catches as a second driver honks the horn while whizzing past me, way over the speed limit and infuriatingly costing me time.

It's too late. The woman rounded the corner that I'm not even close to approaching, and now I'm left with the brand-new worry of a stalker and one looming question that will invade my every thought until I someday get an answer.

Who the hell is she?

Chapter 2
Ruby

THAT WAS A CLOSE ONE.

I never did expect Lizzie to see me, much less to pursue me up the street. It's possible I just made matters even worse by running away from her, but there's no sure way to tell. How would it have gone if I'd simply approached her and said what needed to be said? How quickly would I have got what I wanted if I had taken the direct approach?

We'll never know.

What I *do* know is that I've been pushing my luck. Nobody was ever supposed to see me. The entire operation was designed to be discreet in nature, with me sitting by myself and watching from a distance for the right moment.

I've already blown it.

Lizzie isn't even the first person to see me. That old fool stopped to ask me some questions yesterday. Apparently, I was 'out of place' on that street, which led to a few questions about who I was and what my intentions were.

Needless to say, I ignored him.

Now, here we are. I'm catching my breath in a small lane that's littered with dead, orangey-brown leaves and a faint smell that I reckon has to be pee. My breath comes and goes in small clouds that expel from my mouth like steam. All the while, I just watch.

If Lizzie rounds this corner in a few seconds, there's no telling what I'll say. I suppose I could lie my way through, but what would that achieve? From my days of observation, it's plain to see how protective she is of herself, not to mention her daughter.

So I wait, doubled over with my hands on my knees as I fear the worst. Time crawls by so slowly it's become painful. I check my watch – a tattered old thing I found on the street ten years ago and have kept with me ever since.

Five minutes have passed.

I'm safe.

But that doesn't mean I'm finished. This task

absolutely *will* be carried out in the coming days, and there ain't a damn thing anyone can say or do about it. And if some stupid individual out there dares to intervene?

It's their funeral.

Longwell Green is a quiet area on the east fringe of Bristol. It's the kind of place that's mostly housing, an ideal place to settle down with a family, but there's not much to do unless you enjoy drinking coffee or playing sports. I don't like either of those things.

I just like sex and money.

More specifically, sex *for* money.

Yes, I'm a prostitute. Occasionally, at least. Times have become harder over the years, and a working girl is all I ever was. I was doing it from the tender age of sixteen, and I'm technically still doing it twenty years later. There were breaks in between where other things were going on, but that's the same with most jobs. At the end of the day, nothing has changed.

A whore is whore... is a whore.

But I'm not here to talk about that. I'm not one of those people whose jobs form most of their identity. In fact, it's just something I fell into. I'm planning to get out, too, but not yet. I haven't planned much of my future at all, to be honest. However my current plan works out will determine the next few years of my life, so let's just see how it goes.

I sit in the local café, which, as far as I can tell, used to be a chapel. It's designed that way, at the very least. The women behind the counter are bubbly and loud but in a pleasant way. Heads turn my way as I walk in, some smiling at me as if I'm one of them, while others let their gazes roll up and down my clothes. So what if they're a bit tattered? I've fallen on some rough times and am simply embracing who I am. It's none of their business.

I order an Americano and sit by the window. It takes all of twenty seconds for a man in his fifties to approach me, his dark beard messy and speckled with hints of grey like someone flicked a paintbrush at it. He shrugs off his coat and pulls out a chair, inviting himself to sit at my table before my coffee even arrives. His grubby little hand comes out to shake mine. I'm not sure what attracted him to me – maybe I have a stench of sex about me.

For a fifty-pound note, he could, too.

'Phil,' he says, as if I should already know him.

Hesitantly, I take his hand and smile politely.

It's vital that I come across well, so I tell him my name. Now, before I say it, you should be warned that it will one hundred per cent sound like a prostitute's name. I'd even agree with you.

'Ruby Wishes,' I say, pretending I don't notice his half-smirk.

'Do you live around here?'

'Sort of.'

'What kind of answer is that?'

'The only one you're getting.'

The truth is, my current address is wherever it needs to be. I'm ashamedly living out of my car, which often means I work from home, too. That probably sounds tacky and undesirable, but you'd be shocked at how many people pay extra to do it in a car on a public street. I think they're addicted to the risk.

I'm just addicted to the money.

A mug smashes. An old lady screams. We both turn our heads to the drama, which is basically one of the waitresses running over to tell her it's okay and start clearing it up. The lady who's sitting down – a well-dressed woman who has to be in her sixties – thanks her and apologises profusely. There's nothing else to see here, so Phil and I return to our chat.

'That's Wendy Darling,' he says, pausing while I strain to figure out why it sounds so familiar. 'It's a character from Peter Pan. She lost her marbles a few years ago when her whole family died in a fire. After that, she fell into lunacy. Changed her name. I think to reconnect with her childhood – a time before she had her own family.'

'Right.'

I glance over at the woman and see swirls of sadness in her eyes. I can't imagine what it must be like to lose everyone in your life. The most I've ever lost is one person, and that was hard enough. If I were capable of feeling sympathy, I'd be feeling it right now.

Phil continues to make random, uninteresting conversation that I can't even pretend to be drawn in by. Mostly because a certain character passes by the window. It's his wispy, cloud-like hair I recognise first and then instantly see his angry, accusing face.

'Who's that?' I ask, interrupting Phil and pointing through the glass.

'The old man? That's Ed Warner. Why?'

Because it's good to know your enemies, I think but don't say. My focus remains fixed on Ed until he's out of view, and I start to wonder just how much of a problem he's going to be. I comfort myself by trying to remember that, just like other problems, he can be eliminated.

At long last, the waitress who recently cleaned up the mess plonks an Americano down in front of me. I thank her and continue to engage in useless chit-chat. Over time, some of Phil's friends come to join us at the table. When he figures out he's not getting into my pants without a thick wad of cash, he soon gives up and leaves, waving goodbye to everyone as if he sees them every day. I'm left with two old ladies who are keen to talk about themselves. That's fine by me because all I have to do is nod occasionally and make the odd comment.

Before I know it, they think I'm a good person.

They couldn't be more wrong.

See, I've done things in my life. You don't really know me too well yet, but you've probably already got the sense that I put survival over morals. In the words of the infamous Vanilla Ice, 'If there's a problem, yo, I'll solve it', but I'll do it on my own terms with my own best interests taken care of. Screw everyone else.

What have they ever done for me?

I stick around for another coffee and enjoy the company. Soon, people will start talking about the new stranger in town and how nice she seems. Every little bit helps, doesn't it? Especially when it's all part of a greater scheme to get what I want.

Like I said, I'll do whatever it takes.

From my understanding, it's the last day of school. Which means it's going to be so much easier to keep an eye on both Lizzie and her daughter because they'll always be together. I don't know how that will change when Chris comes home from work, but this will do for now.

I'm currently shrouded in darkness, occupying the front seat of the address I spoke about before (something I like to call 2003 Ford Mondeo Street). The Hughes residence is right across the road, with just two lights on in the entire house. Downstairs, in what I'm guessing is the living room, Lizzie paces back and forth with a paperback in her hand. Her thin, gangly figure is hunched over as she walks into furniture again and again.

Upstairs, there's nothing to see. From my position in the car, all that's visible is some pink wallpaper and the corner of a poster I can't identify. It makes me wonder what kind of person this little Amy is. What kind of music does she like? What foods does she crave versus what she would spit out? Is she kind and friendly or a bully?

And how easy would it be to snatch her from her bed?

Sighing, I shift uncomfortably in my seat and look away. I can't think like that. My thoughts are becoming as dark as the current night sky, and that's dangerous. Darkness leads to desperation, and desperation will blow up everything I've worked for.

That's if Ed Warner doesn't get there first.

I've already identified him as a potential problem, but at least I've already worked myself in with some of the locals. I've got their names and left my impression, which should go a very long way to proving I'm worth having around. Or that I won't cause trouble, in any case.

But I'm getting ahead of myself. This is all just planning and preparation, the same as you might tackle a gardening or DIY project. Groundwork, if you will, to ensure the survival of whatever I build atop it. And, believe me, I have plans to build.

For now though, I just need to get a good night's sleep. It's easier said than done in a cold car though. I don't want to turn on the engine and give myself any heat, mostly because it will draw attention to me and ruin everything. But also, if my battery dies, I'll be totally screwed.

It occurs to me then that anything could derail my entire plan. I'll have to rethink my strategy – maybe even consider making myself known before I'm caught. Would that really be the worst thing in the world? A bit like when someone lies and tries to get their side of the story in first, I could easily approach Lizzie and tell her who I am.

But there's time for that. I'll let it sit for the night and decide for sure in the morning. Until then, I simply need to recline my seat and assure myself that it's all going to work out in my favour. Soon, I'll have everything I want.

Even if everyone else loses.

Chapter 3
Lizzie

NOT ONLY DID I sleep through my alarm, but so did Amy. That would obviously bother me on a school day, but that's not a problem for the next week or so. I have nine full days of childcare to worry about now. It sounds like I'm moaning, but I'm really not.

Amy is the centre of my life.

We start the day as we would any other Saturday. That means a cooked breakfast with bacon, sausages, eggs, and more. The smell wafts through the house in spite of the extractor fan humming on full. My stomach groans at me like an idling truck as the pan hisses up at me. Amy barely looks up from her book, her elbows perched on the kitchen table as she tries to make sense of a story that's three years too advanced for her.

'What do you want to do today?' I ask, buzzing about the kitchen. 'We could—'

'Shh. I'm reading.'

I reel back in exaggerated surprise, widening my eyes with a smirk. It's a pointless effort as her face is still hidden by the spread pages, but it helps as a coping mechanism. What is it they say when a young girl becomes more abrupt? 'She's becoming a real madam?' To be completely honest, I love who she's growing up to be. I just wish she would slow down a little.

By the time the meat is cooked, everything else is prepared. I dish up and tell Amy to put the book away. She obeys with a fed-up roll of the eyes, then thanks me for the effort of making breakfast. That's what I love to see – her manners are rooted firmly in her character.

'Mum...' Amy starts, examining some baked beans on her fork. 'Some of my friends from school said they saw you chasing someone yesterday. Is it true?'

My hand hovers in front of my mouth, the fork gripped tightly in my suddenly tense fingers. How much does she know, exactly? How much *should* she know?

'What are the kids saying?' I ask, putting out the feeler.

Amy shrugs. 'Just that you ran after someone.'

'Do they know who I was chasing?'

'No, but the teachers were talking about it.'

'What did they say?'

'They don't know who it was either.'

I lower my fork as Amy goes on eating. My appetite has suddenly disappeared, but my relationship with (or rather, love for) food makes me feel guilty about shoving my plate to one side. It's such a wasted opportunity to add a couple of pounds to my thin figure.

'Amy, have you noticed anything strange lately?'

'Like what?'

'Like someone following you? Maybe feeling less alone than you should?'

'Not really.'

'Nothing out of the ordinary at all?'

'I said no, Mum. Can I finish eating?'

I smile in spite of how I feel, then tell her that of course she can keep eating. There should be some comfort in how confident she is that nobody has followed her around. Then again, she is only five. What do kids of that age really know?

Looks like I'll have to continue being careful after all.

When she's finished with her breakfast, Amy goes straight back to reading her book. I start clearing up, scraping the contents of my plate into the bin and wishing for the first time in years that I had a dog to feed it to. It would also offer more companionship while Chris is driving across the UK, but it would obviously mean more responsibility. With how chaotic things have been lately, that's the last thing I need.

After breakfast, Amy disappears upstairs while I pull my laptop out in the living room. The plan is to find something fun to do today, but I'm quickly distracted by some social media notifications. There's nothing that steals my interest, but I'm a sucker for keeping a clean and tidy inbox. I guess I'm as anal about that as I am my home's cleanliness.

Just as I clear off the final notification, there's a knock on the door. I thank the gods above for the interruption because as soon as this is dealt with, I can go back to planning our little girls' trip to the forest or something.

Except it doesn't get that far. No sooner do I open the door than my knees go weak. I inhale a sharp breath and step forward, wedging myself between the door and its frame. Our eyes lock, and suddenly, all my fears are standing on my doorstep.

In the shape of the woman who's been following me.

It's hard to get the words out. Instinctively, I take a step back and glance at the stairs, ensuring Amy is not within this woman's sight. When I'm finally able to speak, very little comes out.

'You've been following me,' I state bluntly, recognising that straw-like red hair.

'Lizzie' is all she says until a few highly uncomfortable seconds have passed. Only then does she fold her arms, shift her weight to the other foot, and add, 'I reckon it's about time you and me had a conversation, grown-up to grown-up.'

You and I, dum-dum, I think but bite my tongue. I find my hand has been clutching at my trouser leg, and then I release it and lean against the door frame like a barricade.

'You're damn right we need to talk,' I say. 'You can start by telling me why the hell you've been following me. If it were just the once, I might have thought you simply mistook me for someone else. But considering you just used my name, I'm guessing you know more about me than I know about you.'

'Let's fix that.' The woman offers a pale hand, wrinkled by the cold. 'Ruby Wishes.'

'I'm sure she does. Put your hand down and tell me why you're here.'

'Isn't it obvious?'

'Not to me. Spit it out or get off my property.'

While she stares at me with those blue-grey eyes, I start to question my safety. I was never much of a fighter, and this woman clearly looks like she grew up on the streets – if the frayed clothing doesn't suggest as much, her loose tongue does the rest. What if Chris were here right now? Would I be brave enough to probe further and get to the bottom of this mystery?

Ruby straightens up, unfolds her arms, and places both hands on her hips. When she opens her mouth, the mystery is immediately resolved. But another stands in its place, snaking through the earth like a wicked vine and rooting me to the spot.

'I'm here for Amy,' she says matter-of-factly. 'I'm her birth mother.'

. . .

I've never felt such an odd combination of emotions at once. There's shock at the sheer fact this is happening at all, shame that I didn't figure this out, and overwhelming embarrassment that my reaction is to push the door open wider as if she has a right to enter my home.

Ruby steps inside before I can tell her I made a mistake. I'm assaulted by her sugary-sweet perfume as she comes to stand beside me, shrugging and smiling in a weirdly friendly way. I begin to struggle with the panic of losing my daughter.

'I'm not here for that,' Ruby says as if reading my mind.

'Here for what?'

We both spin around to gaze at the figure on the stairs. Amy is standing there with her book clutched under one arm, a half-drunk glass of water held in her other hand. I hear Ruby's sudden, sharp intake of breath as I try to steady my own. Before I know it, I'm rushing to control the situation before our visitor can get a word in.

'Go back to your room, Little Goof. We need some privacy.'

Amy pulls a face at her nickname, but she

doesn't argue. She turns on her heel and runs back up the stairs, making all the sounds of a jackhammer. Ruby and I are then left by the front door, my head as messy as it was only seconds ago. Perhaps even more.

'Should we...?' Ruby suggests, pointing at the living room.

'No. Let's go to the kitchen.' *It's less invasive.*

I go straight for the mug tree, taking two off with shaking hands and trying to keep myself composed. With the flick of a switch, the kettle starts bubbling the water, which gives me a minute or so to compose myself and figure out what to say. There's no guidebook for things like this. There are laws protecting it but not preventing it.

The kettle finishes its job, and I pour two cups of boiled water. As it splashes into the mugs, I only then realise I haven't put anything else in them. 'God. Um... tea or coffee?'

Ruby comes around the kitchen table and helps herself to a seat. A random shine of sun pours through the nearby window and highlights her messy copper hair, making it look like old wool for a fleeting moment. She smiles and shakes her head.

'Neither. Look, you can relax. I know I should have called first. I'm not trying to take Amy away or anything like that. In fact, I shouldn't be here at all. You can kick me out at any time, and I won't kick up a stink.'

I nod, appreciating it. 'Okay. So why *are* you here?'

She shrugs and leans back, folding her arms again. 'Life hasn't been the easiest for me, but I'm trying to make things right. There's some kind of mental blocker on that while the wound is still open after giving up my only child. I thought... I don't know.'

'That if you can close the wound, then you can move on with your life?'

'Probably something like that, yeah.'

'So what exactly are you asking me?'

'If I can maybe meet her.'

'And how might that go? I don't want to tell her she's adopted.'

'For sure. I wouldn't make you do that either. Maybe we can just say hello?'

I take a deep breath and try to calm myself. While I mull that over, I realise I'm not ready for caffeine but badly need hydration. I pour myself a glass of water from the BRITA filter and down it in one go. Obviously, I was thirstier than I had time to notice.

'Why would I risk that? What is it you think I owe you?'

'You don't owe me anything. I'm just asking for help.'

'Right. So... why would I help someone who followed me and *my* daughter?' I put an unintentional emphasis on 'my', and there are no two guesses as to why – I'm feeling like a super-protective mumma bear.

'Sorry I did that. I just didn't know what else to do. It was hard enough just finding you.'

'How *did* you find me?'

'Your name popped up on social media. I recognised it and explored.'

To be honest, I feel massively violated. Not in the get-your-hand-off-my-leg sense, but in that my home and personal life both feel aggressively invaded. I'm making a mental note right now to change my privacy settings on all the social media apps.

Maybe even delete some.

Ruby screeches her chair back then, standing up with her head down like she's truly ashamed of herself. 'Yeah, I made a mistake coming here. I'm real sorry. I just... sorry. All I wanted was a chance to meet her and see that she's doing well. I'll get out of your hair now.'

Without another word, she pulls the handbag strap up her shoulder and makes her way to the door. There was a break in her voice over those last few words, and suddenly, I'm swaddled in sympathy. I couldn't imagine losing Amy, and something inside me has suddenly triggered to remind me that – this woman? – she already *did* lose her.

'Wait,' I say without thinking.

Ruby stops, turns, and meets my gaze. I hold it for a few moments while I give the decision my best consideration. The problem is, as usual, I speak far faster than I think.

'Tomorrow,' I say in a breath. 'Come back tomorrow. It will be a one-off supervised visit. I'll be right at her side the whole time. You don't tell her who you really are, and you leave as soon as I tell you to. Those are my terms. Take them or leave them.'

It's no surprise when Ruby starts beaming. She rushes across the kitchen, making me flinch. I take a short step back and bump against the kitchen counter, but then she's already on me. Her arms come out and wrap around me, her body pressed against mine as she sobs gratefully onto my shoulder. She smells just like the average street smells: dirty and old and used by many. I wonder if that's where she came from.

If she dares to threaten our family's peace, that's where she'll end up.

Chapter 4
Ruby

THERE AIN'T no way I can describe what I'm feeling right now.

Lizzie gave me a chance!

To be completely honest, I didn't see that coming in a month of Sundays. Like I said, I've been watching her for a while now – way more than I led her to believe – and if there's one thing I learned about her, it's that she doesn't want to share her daughter.

Not that she has a choice.

See, although I'm Amy's birth mother, giving her up for adoption was one big, stupid mistake that I made purely due to my circumstances. The years following what can only be described as the most depressing day of my life have been the hardest of all. Getting paid for sex isn't the most glamorous job in the world, but it puts food in my mouth.

Among other things.

Having said that, I'm in no better position than I was back then – my wallet is only slightly thinner than my waistline, and I'm starting to look ill. What I need is a few good meals, some real sleep in an actual bed, and a little joy from that daughter of mine.

Is that so much to ask?

Apparently not. Lizzie bought into my sweet little persona, as foolishly as expected. It sucks that I have to wait a whole day to see Amy, and it's even worse that it will be a supervised visit, but that doesn't mean I can't plant a seed or two. Even now, as I walk away from the Hughes residence, I'm plotting against Lizzie. That's what you get for taking someone's daughter away from her, I suppose.

I'm still being watched though. I know this because *I* would be watching, so I just keep walking down the street, past Ed Warner (who is standing in his window and twitching at the curtain, staring daggers at me), and round the corner out of sight. I leave my car behind because I don't want Lizzie seeing what I drive. Not yet, anyway.

It would make it so much harder to spy on her.

But that's for another time. Tomorrow, actually. Right now, I have something else to do, and just like every other part of the plan, I'm going to execute it with great patience and a slight touch of deviousness.

That's the only way to get what I want.

THESE ARE the contents of my purse:

One hundred and seventeen pounds, thirteen pence. A half-empty pack of spearmint gum that's been there so long the foil has faded and thinned. An old phone fit for calls, texts, and some social media if you give it enough time to load. The charger to go with it. Three condoms of different sizes and sensitivities. A penknife, just in case.

I've only had to use the latter once... so far.

But today, I'll be spending some of the spare cash on a trip into Bristol's city centre. I'll use it sparingly without neglecting the whole purpose of my trip, which is to buy some clothes that don't stink like a skunk's bum. I want to leave a good impression on Amy, even if she doesn't know that I'm her real mother.

Yet.

I take a bus to save on petrol and kill some time. I'm in no hurry to get back to my car anyway, so I leave it on Lizzie's street and hopefully wind up the old fella who lives nearby. I get a certain satisfaction from upsetting people who've done me wrong, and daring to question my presence on the street was... let's just say 'offensive'.

The bus stops, hisses, and jolts. I step off and into the warm sun, soaking it in before I step out of everyone's way. I've been here before – not in years, but not much has changed – and make my way through to the Cabot Circus mall. If memory serves, the top floor plays host to all the expensive eateries, the middle floor has a random selection of businesses such as coffee shops and toy shops, and the lower ground is an equally but larger mishmash of outlets. It's mostly clothes, and only every other shop has affordable items.

I try my luck in one of the smaller places, using the price tags on the mannequins in the window as an indicator that I can afford something if I'm minimalist, which shouldn't be too hard. I usually run the cliché of attending work in a revealing top and miniskirt, but today, I'm looking for something warmer. Something that doesn't say I'm trashy.

It doesn't take long to find what I want. There's a pair of jeans for only fifteen pounds, three sets of panties and socks for just under six, and a simple T-shirt with a picture of a surfer on the front. That one costs less than a Big Mac meal, so I snatch it off the rack and put it up against me. Satisfied, I take a quick look at the coat section, decide it's worth splashing for something clean and warm, then take it all to the till. The overall cost is not as damaging as I thought it would be, but I don't like the cold eye the assistant is giving me.

I wouldn't mind plucking it out with my penknife.

But I won't, of course. I'm not loony on my better days, and this is one of those. I put aside my bitter resentment and leave the shop with my bag. I'm actually pleased with my purchases, but I won't put them on until tomorrow. No point risking making them stink, right?

I'm just starting to think about grabbing some food when the phone buzzes in my handbag. I shift all my belongings to take a look at the cracked screen, only to find that *he* is calling me. I sigh, which turns into a light cough, then reject the call.

It was pretty naïve of me to think it would end there. I've barely made it thirty steps before I have another missed call and two text messages. I check them quickly and roll my eyes, trying to stifle the anger rising like a scorching wave in my belly.

They read:

Don't you dare ignore me.

And:

I want updates. NOW!

Well, I don't want to give updates until I'm ready. Just who the hell does he think he is, anyway? Not my boss, that's for sure, and certainly not my man. That's a long-winded way of saying he has absolutely no control over me, so screw him for thinking otherwise.

I heave a heavy breath and continue to the nearest Greggs, where I'll treat myself to something hot and cheap to eat. I'm thinking of a sausage roll and maybe a steaming white coffee. Maybe a doughnut, too, if that will help clear my mind a little. I deserve it, don't I? After all I've done and all that's ahead of me, the least I deserve are a few cheap nummies.

Ah, but it's no use. Even after devouring the food, I can't shake that bastard from my thoughts. There's an intense feeling of mounting pressure there, for sure. Maybe that's why I'm having trouble keeping the baked goods down.

Maybe that's why I feel so sick.

I try filling the rest of the day with a relaxing walk, browsing the tech shops and wondering what it might feel like to afford some of this stuff. I've had clients with a ton of money, their six- or seven-bedroom houses reserved for stuff like this – for games consoles and massive TVs to fill the empty voids in their lives. No wonder they're lonely if they spend all their time at home.

But it works for me. I still get paid.

Over time, I'm starting to feel my mood lift. I'm riddled with anxiety about seeing Amy tomorrow, but it's the good kind. Butterflies, some people call them. I've never felt anything like this before, and I oddly like the sensation.

Not that it lasts long.

My phone is buzzing again just minutes after I find my happy place. I step into an alley where there's nothing but graffiti and large wheelie bins, then reject the call once more. This time though, I quickly send a text because I'm starting to panic that I'm upsetting him. It's true that I don't belong to him, but that doesn't mean I'm not afraid of him.

I've made progress. Meeting her tomorrow.

That's all I say, and it's all I *have* to say. Until I get a little closer to my girl, there's nothing left to tell. So I put my phone away and continue walking through the city centre, taking in the subtle sights with just one thought in the back of my throbbing head.

Soon, this will all be over.

ANOTHER NIGHT, another sore back.

The sun is just rising as I stir, the golden rays creeping into the car window like water rising through a sinking ship. When it assaults my eyes, I turn and groan under my breath, using swear words you're better off not hearing as I shudder in the cold.

It's been a long night, mostly because it took me a long time to get to sleep. I've been too anxious, too fed up with how my life is going, but most of all, I've been so crazily excited to see that precious daughter of mine. Every time I tried to close my eyes, all I saw was that sweet little smile – that adorable twinkle she gets in her eye when she's happy.

I want to be the one to give her that twinkle.

Back in the day, I would start every morning by sleeping in and then waking up to a huge mug of coffee while watching TV. Those days died long ago, when I spent all of my money and drank the rest. We all make mistakes, and that was yet another one of my epic blunders. Now, my only option is to sit in this bloody car with my breath exploding into a foggy cloud in front of me, waiting for the early risers to pass so I can get dressed in the back seat.

When the coast is clear, I sneak through the front seats and into the rear of my car. Then I play a little game I like to call 'slip it in sneakily'. Usually this game is best played with a client, but today, the 'it' is my arm, and all it's slipping into is a sleeve. I'm well-practised in this stuff, but that's not to say it's easy – my car ain't a big one, and my joints are too stiff from the cold to go bending this way and that. That's why it takes so bloody long.

After finally changing into the clothes I bought

yesterday, I check my phone to see if *he* has messaged me. Thankfully, he's left me to do what needs to be done. It's just as well, seeing as the battery is dying a slow and painful death. I gotta remember to charge this thing.

The next couple of hours are spent gnawing on my nails as I gaze up at Lizzie's house. At *Amy's* house. This whole thing could come crashing to the ground at any moment, so it's vital I stay on my best behaviour. As much as I can, anyway. I still have things that need doing.

When I finally summon the courage, I step out of the car, check both ends of the street to see they're empty, then head towards the house. It's a big place. Fancy, too. Clean on the inside, but you wouldn't guess from the bland gravel path up to the front door. The one I knock on with anxiety burning through my veins like acid.

There's no telling how this is going to go. As I stand here and wait to meet my daughter – properly this time – I can't help thinking this is something we both deserve. I need to be with Amy, and she needs to be with me.

Everyone else can go to hell.

Chapter 5
Lizzie

For all the sleep I didn't get last night, I might as well have been doing it upside down.

It wasn't the nerves that got to me, but the guilt – the question of why I'm allowing this to happen when it's such a huge risk to the stability of our little family. It's for sympathy, I suppose. *Empathy*, at the very least. I know that if I'd had to give my baby away, I would want to meet her years later. That is, *meet* her.

The line is drawn right there.

I've seen where this goes. I've watched dads cry when handing their kids back to the mother after a weekend. I've seen mums drop their kids off at school for the first day and sit in the car crying for the next few hours. Parents always want more.

As a mother myself – non-biologically or otherwise – I can appreciate that.

It's a little after nine when Ruby comes knocking. Amy still doesn't know what's about to happen, and I'd like to keep it that way until the ground rules are firmly set. Boundaries that absolutely must be agreed upon. As far as I know, anyway. This is my first time.

I open the door to a woman who's dressed completely differently from the last time I saw her. Ruby's wearing jeans and a neat new coat that reaches her knees. The whole get-up is super-casual, but mainly, it looks clean. And even though her hair is still frayed and wiry, she's made an effort to brush it into a ponytail. It's such a drastic change. A pleasant one.

'Good morning,' I say dully, sounding more defensive than intended.

'All right? Can I come in?'

I shove open the door and step aside, shutting out the cold whisper of wind that tries following her in. Ruby shivers as it touches her, then wraps her arms around her shoulders as her gaze roams the hallway. It's like she's never seen the inside of the house before.

'Where is she?' she asks.

'Hold on a moment.' I stand up tall and try to be assertive. *Try*. 'Before you go anywhere near Amy, we need to establish a few rules. Firm ones. And if you don't agree to every last one of them, you can turn around and go back right this second.'

'That's fair enough.' Ruby assesses me with cold eyes. 'Let's hear them.'

'For starters, you are under no circumstances to tell her who you are.'

'How am I supposed to—?'

'*No* circumstances.'

Ruby shrinks into herself. I suck it up and continue.

'If I get even the slightest hint that you're a danger to her, I'll be contacting the police. If you even start acting like she's your daughter rather than mine, this little act of kindness will come to an abrupt end. Do we understand each other?'

'I mean...' She scratches the back of her neck and looks away. 'Of course.'

Something about the way she says it leads me to think she's not trustworthy. My gut instinct is to cancel this whole thing right now, but I've already come too far. It feels as though telling her to turn around and walk away would be nothing less than sheer cruelty. Besides, she's agreeing to these things. Isn't that what I wanted?

'Anything else?' she asks awkwardly.

'Yes. This won't last for very long. You talk to her, say goodbye, then leave.'

Ruby visibly swallows, nodding like she's not entirely happy but will not disrespect the rules. That's good enough for me, and it's only made better when she opens her mouth to talk. 'I just want you to know I'm really grateful for this. You won't have to worry about anything. I'll respect your wishes. Trust me.'

Even now, as I stare into her eyes, it feels like something might be slightly off. The words she used sounded completely genuine, so I have no rational reason to deprive her of the thing she craves the most. Along with that, I also keep wondering how I would feel in her situation – of course I would want more than one short meeting.

But she's agreeing, isn't she?

'Good,' I say, gesturing towards the living room. 'Then let's get this over with.'

There are two sofas in our living room, each facing the other, with a coffee table in the centre.

Ruby takes the one further from the door, which I'm glad about. It means that Amy can have a quick exit if she doesn't feel comfortable, and that's how we raised her.

I find her upstairs, sitting on her bed surrounded by dolls and books. She's cross-legged, her hair dangling over her eyes as she narrates to her lifeless buddies. I watch her for a moment, almost feeling guilty for what I'm about to put her through, then remind myself that she has nothing to fear.

As long as Ruby stays true to her word.

'Can you come downstairs, Little Goof?'

'Don't call me—'

'Sorry. Come on, I'd like you to meet someone.'

Amy scrunches up her face, rolls her eyes, then climbs her way off the bed. Her feet catch a couple of Barbies and knock them to the floor. She hesitates, probably thinking about picking them up, but doesn't delay any further.

Before we know it, we're entering the living room together. Ruby's eyes light up, her face transforming with the smile that spreads across it. She moves to stand as Amy comes in and sits on the sofa across from her. I shoot her a look that makes her stop. She sits back.

'This is a friend of mine,' I explain to my daughter. 'Her name is Ruby.'

Amy nods like a formal adult in a social situation, then extends her hand. 'It's ever so nice to meet you, Ruby. My name is Amy Hughes. It's a pleasure to make your acquaintance.'

Ruby grins, and I laugh out loud.

'She picks up a lot from TV,' I say.

'That's okay. I like TV, too.' Ruby leans on her elbows. 'What do you enjoy watching?'

'Hmm. Mostly cartoons.'

'Me, too. Which is your favourite?'

'*Adventure Time* and *Sesame Street*.'

Ruby interweaves her fingers and lays her chin on her fists, her smile broadening. 'You know, *Sesame Street* was around when I was a little girl. I always loved Elmo, but Cookie Monster makes me laugh every time.'

Amy's jaw drops, and suddenly, she looks her age again. 'I *love* Cookie Monster!'

'You do?'

'Yeah!'

I take a few steps back, eased slightly into the idea that this might not be the worst thing in the world. It's not like I'm going out of earshot, but if it makes them both feel more comfortable around each other, then who am I to intrude? Amy seems to like her, and Ruby would... well, Ruby is biologically designed to like her daughter.

My daughter.

Sickness unsettles my stomach at the mistake, even though I didn't express it out loud. Looking at this couple is like night and day, physically speaking, but they're meeting in the middle to make sunrise. Amy is on her feet, leaning against Ruby and giggling at something she said, and Ruby looks over at me occasionally as if to tell me everything will be okay. I appreciate the comfort, and it almost makes me like her.

Almost.

The two of them continue to talk for almost an hour. It does hurt to watch, but it's important to remind myself that this isn't about me. It's about Amy meeting her real mum, and someday, I might even be able to tell her the truth about her heritage – that she may have been raised a Hughes, but she was born a Wishes.

I scoff at the silly surname as if to defend myself from what I'm feeling. Ruby and Amy both look up at me, and I realise I'm staring. I shake my head and apologise, then suggest that they break apart. Amy complains, but Ruby tells her it's okay.

'I had a lot of fun meeting you,' she says. 'Would it be out of order to ask for a hug?'

Amy looks at me. Ruby's eyes follow. There's nothing intrusive or entitled about it. It's only then that I understand she wasn't asking for Amy's permission.

She was asking for mine.

'If it's okay by Amy, it's okay by me.'

Amy doesn't hesitate. She spreads her arms and slams into Ruby's chest. Ruby laughs as the wind leaves her, hugging her in return and enjoying the five- to ten-second embrace that's killing me inside. All I keep thinking is that she's *my* little girl. Is that selfish?

When they've said goodbye, Amy returns upstairs, barely missing the waterworks. Ruby apologises to me in the silence, rummaging in her handbag for tissues she can't find. I hand her the box from the coffee table, for which she thanks me, dabs her eyes, then gets up to leave.

'I can't thank you enough for this,' she says, and it sounds like it comes from the heart. 'Sorry for intruding on your home, and well done for raising her the way you did. She's just the loveliest little girl, ain't she?'

'She is.'

'Take good care of her, okay?'

I catch myself nodding as I show her the door. My hostility vanished a long time ago, back when I finally understood exactly how important the meeting was for this woman. Maybe I helped close a wound somehow. I hope she'll feel better about her life soon enough, and that sudden bout of empathy makes me feel bad as Ruby Wishes leaves this house for the last time.

LATER THAT NIGHT, after a whole day of trying to re-establish my own bond with Amy, I'm lying on my bed with a book. I'm not really into it because my mind is all over the place, like some bomb just hit it and scattered my thoughts everywhere. As you can imagine, I'm scrambling around like a crazy person trying to gather them all.

But the feeble attempt comes to an abrupt end when my phone rings.

I snatch it up and answer as soon as I see who it is. Chris rarely calls me while he's working, so it's a delight when he does check in. The book drops to the duvet, and I sit up, my entire body riveting with excitement.

'About time you called,' I say.

'Good evening to you, too. How is everything?'

'It's all good. Except there has been a... strange development.'

'Has the rash come back?'

'What? No. Gross.'

It's not the easiest thing to explain, but I give it my all. Chris doesn't say a word while I tell him all about Ruby – about how she's already come in and met her daughter. *Our* daughter, I remind myself again. By the time I'm finished telling him, it feels as though I've relived it all over again. Every conflicting emotion comes back for another pass.

'Let me get this straight,' Chris says, sounding unnaturally stressed. 'A suspicious woman started following you around, eventually introduced herself as our daughter's birth mother, who was never officially identified, and you made the not-too-smart decision to invite her in and meet Amy?'

'Well, when you put it like that...'

'You didn't think her father would want a say in this?'

I clap a hand to my mouth. My first thought is to bite back at him and express that I'm a grown woman who can make her own decisions. But he's right – that was a very bad move on my part, and the least I can do is take responsibility for it.

'God, you're right,' I say. 'I'm so sorry.'

'What were you thinking?'

'Perhaps I was just so swept up in the confusion of it all that I didn't know what to do.' My heart is racing. It takes a lot for Chris to get upset with me, so I have to take it seriously when he does. 'I don't know what to say. I messed up big time, and I'll do whatever it takes to make it up to you. Can you forgive me?'

There's a long, uncomfortable silence. I spend the time trying to gauge just how upset he is. Before I can reach a decision, the question answers itself. I don't need to ask him how he feels because he's just made it very clear by doing something he's never done before.

He hangs up.

Chapter 6
Before...

WAY BACK THEN – in a time when I had a small flat and plenty of repeat business – life seemed a little less complicated. I had a pimp, the kind you see in films with rotten teeth and an overprotective nature, but he kept his distance for the most part. His main job was to work as a middleman. He'll send someone over to 'go to town' on me, and in return, I'd give him a cut of the profits. I enjoyed my job at the time, so I worked a lot.

It really hit a speed bump on a busy Saturday. There was a total of eight men that day (if you count it from midnight to midnight) and a few more on the Sunday. Don't get me wrong, all of my clients used condoms. It was one of the rules. If they broke the rule, my pimp broke their face and then some. It was a fair deal. Everyone stuck to it.

After the final person left, I scrubbed myself harder than ever before, slipped into some clean clothes, and lay down on the sofa with my knees brought up to my chest. I never felt ashamed of what I did for a living, but every now and then, I felt a yearning for true love. It's every young girl's dream, ain't it? To grow up and have a fairy-tale wedding with a handsome prince? Somehow, I knew it wasn't on the cards for me.

Especially since I knew I was pregnant.

People later told me how dumb I sounded – that I couldn't possibly know I had a bun in the oven – but I could just feel *it. The same way you know you've got a flat tyre or that the bus you're waiting for came and went long before you stood at the stop. It took a few weeks for me to take a test, but when I did, it came out positive.*

But was 'positive' the right word? I wasn't sure what to feel. Excitement? Relief? I was a dirty little prostitute living in the more shameful end of Bristol, without much to my name and no prospects. To make things worse, there was no telling how I was supposed to get out of this lifestyle. Maybe the baby inside me was my cue. But would my pimp see it that way?

He'd have to.

See, I didn't believe in abortion. I was never about to tell anyone how to live their life, but that kind of stuff just wasn't for me. As long as the baby came to full term and was born healthily, nothing was going to stop me from giving birth to this kid.

It's what came after that scared me.

Chapter 7
Ruby

I CAME across as a pretty decent woman.

So I fooled them pretty well.

It's been two days since my meeting with Amy, and I haven't forgotten a single second of it. It was like I met my best friend or a younger extension of myself, going over our likes and dislikes with a lovely girl who should be mine. Walking away from her for a second time was the hardest thing I ever had to do.

But I'm coming back today.

There's a Halloween fair in a local green that's going to be resplendent with opportunities to bump into Lizzie and Amy. I know they're going because I haven't stopped following them since our last encounter. I've watched, listened, and learned everything I could about their next moves. For instance, Amy is going to be dressed as a witch.

And Lizzie is going to feel sorry for me.

My age-worn clothes are back on, letting her see just how much I'm struggling. There's a chill in the air that makes my nipples feel like little nails, and the goosebumps on my bare legs prick all the way up under my skirt. It's no way to dress – not for a family event – and it's going to draw some eyes. That's fine by me. The more chance of her seeing me, the better.

The fair itself is a pretty nifty event. It's not very big, but there's enough space for a few stalls, a face-painting table, and a seating area for some food. Hot dogs are being grilled nearby – I can't see them, but that lovingly familiar scent makes my stomach grumble. And if you're thinking of a joke about how a hooker loves a sausage, save it. I've heard them all.

Kids are running around in their costumes, their parents tagging along behind. Some of them are dressed up, too. I've seen tons of witches, a few clowns, and more Spider-Mans (Spider-Men?) than I care to count. Just when did superheroes become horror figures anyway?

The cold is getting to me more than the

screaming kids, but I stand my ground and wait patiently. My hands cup my arms as I shudder in the frosty wind. My gaze roams all around the packed-out field as I look for them. It doesn't take too long.

In fact, *they* find *me*.

'Ruby?'

It's Amy's voice, excited and shrill. I rotate my torso slightly to my left, my feet not moving as the cold pins my feet to the mud. She's standing nearby, an Elsa dress lazily hidden under a puffy winter coat. Lizzie is just a few paces behind her with a stunned expression of curiosity. She didn't expect to see me here.

Good.

'Hey, how are you doing?' I ask Amy, bending over slightly as she bounds over like a baby deer. 'I was just checking out the fair. Didn't realise you two were coming?'

'We've got sweets!' She lifts a bag packed to the brim with sugary treats. 'Want one?'

'No, thank you. But it's very kind that you offered.' I stand up straight and address Lizzie. No point in upsetting her, is there? That will, in turn, upset my entire plan. 'Sorry, I didn't mean to get in the way of you two. I had no idea you'd be here.'

Lizzie raises her chin like she wants to nod, then looks me up and down to figure out whether I'm lying. I guess this is another win for me. 'Nah, it's fine. Amy, why don't you go and get us all hot dogs? Three in total. No mustard on mine.'

'Oh, wow. Are you sure?' I ask.

'It's no bother.'

'Thank you.'

Amy takes a twenty-pound note and disappears between the stalls. I briefly think how easy it would have been to just snatch her and run, but that's not the kind of person I am... is it? Maybe it is, maybe it isn't, but I wouldn't get far. Not with Lizzie right behind me.

'I really didn't realise you'd be here,' I plead when we're alone. 'If you want, I can go away and come back to explore later when you're gone. The last thing I want to do is force myself into your plans for the day.'

'Relax.' Lizzie smiles. 'How were you to know?'

'You're too good to me.'

'Probably. Did you change your clothes again?'

'Yeah, they didn't suit me. I took them back for a refund.'

'I thought you looked nice in them.'

That comment makes me pause. I'm not used

to compliments outside of how big my boobs are or how good I am on top, so it's hard to accept. It does make me smile though – I did nothing to deserve such a nice comment, but I liked it.

'Why don't you hang out with us?' Lizzie says finally, just like I wanted her to.

'No, I couldn't. She's your daughter.'

'But you're here alone, aren't you?'

'Yeah.'

'Then I won't take no for an answer. Come on, let's go get that hot dog and have a nice day before you go back home. Just don't tell my husband.' She smiles and puts a hand on my shoulder, and we walk in the direction Amy vanished in. It's a relief to know how little effort it takes to work her like a puppet.

I wonder how soon I can cut her strings.

We spend the afternoon like a dream. There are skittles competitions, a coconut shy, and even a small play by some of the local kids. It's their own version of *Casper the Friendly Ghost*, which is far from charming. See, I'm one of those people who doesn't like kids...

Except for my own.

We leave the fair early as per Amy's demands, heading straight for the park, which is at least a fifteen-minute walk towards their home. Just to help sell the appearance that I'm sweet and unintrusive, I offer to part ways with them. I do it right in front of Amy because I know damn well what her reaction will be.

I'm right, too.

'No!' she yells and grabs my hand like I'm suddenly her best friend. 'Can't Ruby come?'

I shy away but look to Lizzie, asking for her permission without speaking a single word. It's easy to see the struggle in her eyes, but she does her best not to show it. Her deliberation turns into a smile, and she agrees it's not a bad idea.

During our journey, Amy runs ahead. It gives me and her mother – her adoptive mother, that is – a chance to talk. Rubbing my hands together in the cold, I continue down the path and keep my head down. That's the easiest way to communicate.

'You mentioned something about your husband,' I say. 'Would he not approve of me being here? I just don't want to cause any problems in your family.'

'Not really. I told him you came over the other day.'

'What did he say?'

'Let's just say he wasn't happy.'

'I'm sorry. I never meant to create friction. Really.'

'It's not you, it's me.' She laughs at the cliché saying, and I smirk along to it. 'I know my husband very well, and I assumed he would be okay with this. But that's where I went wrong – I made an assumption. And you know what they say about that.'

'No?'

Lizzie glances at me. 'That it makes an "ass" of "u" and "me".'

I knock my head back and cackle like some kind of demon. Although she's looking at me like I'm the last person in the world to hear that, it really is new to me. 'That's a good one. But still, I hope I didn't disrupt your marriage or anything.'

'No, it's fine. Honestly. As long as I stay open with him about what's going on, he'll come around. Like today, for instance. He'd hit the roof if I kept this from him, but doing it in the first place won't upset him too much. The way he'll see it, the damage is already done.'

'It's that simple?'

'Probably.' She sighs. 'Look, why don't you stay for dinner tonight?'

'Oh, no, really, I couldn't.'

'But I insist. To tell the truth, I've been trying to find a way to tell you that you shouldn't interact with Amy any more. Although at the same time, I'm as human as you are. So why don't you just milk it, enjoy the day with us, and then say goodbye?'

'And your husband...?'

'Chris wouldn't mind.'

'Then... thank you.'

I don't say any more, but it does make me wonder if she often decides things on behalf of her husband. It's not nice, but it really does sound like she means well.

For all the good that will do her.

The park is more exhausting than I remember. When I was a kid, I could run around all day and not tire at all. We were running laps and climbing up the slide only to slip back down it again on purpose. Those are the kinds of things we do with Amy, burning her out as much as possible but to no avail. Like I hinted at, her energy is limitless.

One person does get tired though – Lizzie takes a seat on the bench and lets out a breath of exasperation. I get it. Amy takes a lot of work just from the short space of time I'm spending with her today. And I haven't been here very long at all.

Imagine when she's mine again.

As Lizzie starts looking at her phone, I'm alone with Amy by the swings. It takes all of my willpower not to seize the moment and do what I really want to do – to tell her who I really am and offer her to come with me. Would it really be the worst thing in the world? How would Lizzie react, I wonder? Not well, I'll bet.

Back at the house, Lizzie creates an amazing but simplistic meal of curry with rice. It was done in a slow cooker, she says. Whatever that is. I'm just glad to get a full meal in my belly without having to spend some time with a grubby little man. Not only that, but the company is good. We chat and tell jokes and laugh, and it's suddenly like I'm in a real family.

I guess I am, even if only for a couple more hours.

Saying goodbye to Amy for the 'last' time is the hardest. We hug at the door, and then she bounds towards the stairs as if we'll see each other again tomorrow. Who knows – maybe we will. It all depends on how well I execute the next part.

'Thank you so much,' I tell Lizzie as I step out of the house and into the cold. The bitter night breeze gnaws at my skin, and I make a point of letting her see me shiver. 'You've been kinder than anyone I ever knew, so I'll get out of your hair.'

'You're very welcome,' she says. 'Do you have far to go?'

'Erm... a few feet.'

Lizzie cocks her head to one side, puzzled.

Then, as I prepared from the start, I jingle the keys in my hand. 'I have a Mondeo parked up the road. No fixed address, so I guess I'll be heading wherever life takes me. Listen, thanks again for everything. I'll never forget this.'

Before she can get a word in, I walk away. An essential part of the plan is that she doesn't know I'm fishing for more. Nothing bluffs it quite like leaving her on the doorstep. My heart is beating like a drum as I gain more and more distance from her. I half expect her to come running and tell me it's all going to be okay – that I can stay for the night or maybe longer.

Unfortunately, the further I get, the less likely it becomes. I'm off her property and heading out of sight. From a side glance, I catch Ed snooping from behind his curtain again, but my focus is on the reflection in his window. I'm watching Lizzie's front door and Lizzie, who still hasn't gone back inside. It looks hopeful... until she finally shuts it.

Shit.

Chapter 8
Lizzie

HAVE you ever been in one of those moral dilemmas? You know, the ones where the right thing to do is not the *easy* thing to do, and the smallest part of you thinks it's a bad idea? It's like there's a little red light blinking in my head, warning me not to do it.

That's why I closed the door.

Now, let me get one thing straight: that's not me. I'm not the type of person to shut a homeless person out in the cold. Especially if that person is technically family, in a weird, twisted little way. So, as I lean my back against the door and huff out a stressed breath, I can't help but think I'm doing something horribly wrong.

I feel as though I've not given Ruby everything

I can. Her struggle is real, just like mine was when I couldn't conceive all those years ago. As much of a pain in the backside as it was to get through the adoption process without a significant other (I hadn't met Chris yet), Ruby was there, willing to trust me with her only child. And based on what? The things she read on a few sheets of paper back when I worked hard and used the money to buy my own home?

It's not like that any more though.

After adopting Amy, I had to sell all but one of my businesses to stay and be a mother. The thing is, no matter how bad it felt to give up everything I worked for, there was something even better waiting for me at home. That same sense of loss I felt for selling up couldn't compare to what Ruby must have felt when she sent her baby to live with someone else.

So, what kind of person would I be to just let her walk?

Without another thought, my hands quickly reach for the chain. I tear open the door and step into the cold as it bites my bare arms. Despite all my intuitions warning me not to do it, I face the direction Ruby walked in and, immediately regretting it, call out to the birth mother.

'Wait!'

When no voice comes back, I put the latch on the door to keep it from closing, then trudge down the gravel path in my slippers. The air is aggressively icy, so I hug my own chest and peer down the street to where Ruby is unlocking the Ford Mondeo she mentioned earlier.

'Ruby,' I call. 'Hold on.'

She stops and turns, but her figure is all that's visible in the barely lit street. I hurry towards her, passing Ed's house and shooting him an angry look as he peers out of his window. I swear to God, he's such a nice guy, but I'm sick to death of him looking in on my business.

When I reach Ruby, key in hand and looking at me all puzzled, I catch my breath. My muscles seize up in the low temperatures. It makes me wonder how she's survived out here, sleeping in a car in this kind of weather. It's not even winter yet, but it's far from warm.

'Are you really going to sleep out here all night?' I ask.

'That's the plan. Just like any other night.'

'But... why? Don't you have a home?'

'Sort of, but it's not that simple.'

'It's none of my business, although you can tell me if you want.'

'I would only bore you.'

'Honestly, you wouldn't.'

Ruby takes a deep breath. It comes out like a ship's funnel expelling smoke. Her eyes, although barely visible, dart around all over the place as if she's about to tell some grand secret. I'm not going to lie – she has me curious.

'I'm not a good person,' she begins. 'Although I have a feeling I was always meant to be. When I was growing up, I used to read a lot just to escape from the world around me. When my parents argued so loud they annoyed the entire apartment building, I'd turn to TV. But no matter how loud the TV went, it wasn't enough to drown out all the noise.

'When my dad started hitting my mum, I used to try fighting him off. I took a few hits here or there just to protect her, but in the end, she would always come crawling back to him. They would snuggle up on the sofa and act like nothing happened. Until the next time, obviously. But I would be the bad guy in that situation, you know? Like I was the one standing between them all the time, and their hate for me kept growing. I had to get out, and there wasn't a thing on earth I wouldn't do to start a new life.

'My first job was delivering food by hand from a local greengrocer. It ended badly because I was living on the streets and had to steal some food just to survive. I never felt too good about it, but it was the only thing I could do. Anyway, they found out and fired me. Then I was homeless, jobless, and still only sixteen years old.'

I shake my head in surprise. 'You've been homeless since you were sixteen?'

'No, not that long. Because I got lucky and found my feet in sex work.'

'You're a prostitute!' The words tumble out with more judgement than intended.

'A *part-time* prostitute.'

Despite how my outburst made it seem, it's really not all that surprising. I study her from head to toe, examining the cheap clothing and the rough skin – the confidence with which she holds herself, although it's so obviously just a trick to convince herself she's worth something.

My stomach feels uneasy because I let a sex worker near my daughter.

God, I think. *Amy's real mother is a hooker!*

'There was plenty of work,' Ruby continues with a touch of shame in her sad face. 'I earned a lot of money, learned to drive, bought some clothes, and even kept a roof over my head. Nothing fancy, but it was a home. Anyway, Ricky – he was my pimp – started increasing his take on the jobs I did. It got so bad that I was running out of money fast. The only thing I could think to do was meet with some of those clients privately and start seeing them more frequently. Also... do more things with them than I was comfortable with.'

Ruby takes another deep breath.

'I don't know which one was Amy's father. I never will.'

My hand comes to my dry mouth as my heart flutters with shock and sadness. That nauseating feeling comes back, tugging at my soul and making me feel like I'm about to throw up some slow-cooked curry. If you'll excuse the image.

'There was a bit of a market for pregnant whores,' Ruby goes on, 'but not much. Things got so bad that I had to stand up tall and say enough was enough. I went around a little while, taking odd jobs here and there – *real* jobs that didn't involve sex – but they were cash in hand. I wasn't on the books, which worked for me because I lost my home anyway. It's much harder to land a solid job when people want a home address on file.'

'When was this?'

'A couple of years ago.'

'So you've been working from your car ever since?'

'There's been no other choice. I even toured the country a little, following the work up through places like London and Manchester, but soon, the travelling got expensive. I came back to Bristol a couple of months ago, hoping maybe my parents could help me after all these years. But they died twelve years ago, and I never even knew about it.'

As someone whose parents also passed away, I can easily relate to her misery. It's not an easy thing to go through, seeing as the two people most apt to support you during a hard time are the ones who are gone from our lives. With Ruby, it must have been even harder. Her situation was incredibly complicated. Especially emotionally.

'So,' I say. 'Ever since then...?'

'I've just been wandering around doing the part-time sex thing. So no, I don't have a home to go to because both my job and my home are sitting on these four wheels. But in the back of my mind, I always thought life would be okay because I have a little girl out there somewhere. I always wondered what happened to her – what she's like. And you, with all the kindness in your heart, gave me a chance to say hello and goodbye. I'll always remember this.'

I shake my head, already feeling bad about Chris. What will he say when he learns about everything that's happened? I lied to Ruby and told her Chris would be okay with this – he'd be far from it. How will he react when he hears the news of everything I'm about to say to Ruby – the real mother of his precious little girl.

'Stay,' I blurt out.

'What?' Ruby steps back. 'I couldn't.'

'You can, and you will. It's not much, but there's a perfectly good sofa in our living room, and I can leave the heating on downstairs so you don't freeze up. I also can't say how long we can put you up for – maybe a day, maybe a month – but it's something for now.'

'Really, I can't—'

I reach out and snatch her hand into mine. 'You're sleeping in a car, Ruby. It's almost November, you have no job, no money, and nowhere to stay. Things might get complicated, but as long as we can work together around the Amy thing, there's no reason you can't have a roof over your head just for a short while. I won't take no for an answer.'

Ruby beams as I drag her back towards the house, and once again, I get that nagging feeling that I'm doing something wrong. The rational part of my brain says it's impossible – that I'm being a good human being for someone in need.

So then... why is this feeling suffocating me?

I'll soon find out.

Ruby's nightwear is not much different from her day clothes. All she does is slip off the sweater, sit down, and gently rub her arms while looking around the living room. I drop the duvet and pillow beside her. *Flumpf.*

'Something wrong?' I ask.

'Nah. I'm just not used to taking clothes off to go to sleep. It's so cold in the car that I'm usually putting on more layers just so I don't end up ill.'

'Well, you won't have to worry in this house. It's always warm.'

'Thank you. Sincerely, for everything.'

I nod like it's not a bother, but I must admit I'm worried about the impact it's going to have on Amy.

I was even starting to get a little jealous earlier when she and Ruby were playing at the park. I didn't know anything about this woman then, especially as she left her baby in the hospital without revealing her name. But after hearing about what brought her back to Bristol and caused her to end up homeless, I couldn't help feeling sorry for her.

'If you need anything in the night, there's food in the fridge and water in the tap.'

'Where else?' Ruby laughs softly. It's pleasant. 'What time does everyone get up?'

'I'm up at seven every day. I'll try not to wake you.'

'Don't worry about it. It's your home. Be as loud as you want.'

'Sleep well.'

I start to leave, but Ruby stands up to address me. My initial reaction is to stand back for some reason, but there's no telling what makes me do it. Ruby certainly seems like a pleasant person who couldn't say boo to a goose, so I put it down to the nag in my head again.

'Is something wrong?' I ask, wringing my fingers now.

'I just wonder how this will work. With Amy, I mean.'

'Remember those rules we decided on?'

'Yeah.'

'They haven't changed. She'll not know the truth until she's ready. However long that takes, it's not going to be until she's at least sixteen.' Pausing, I take a deep, steadying breath. 'Look, I know how hard it must be for you, but she's my daughter now. I'm compassionate enough to let you stay, but nothing will change when it comes to her.'

Ruby gives two thumbs up with an awkward smile, then returns to sit on the sofa. She starts messing around with the duvet, unfolding it and spreading it over her legs. 'You don't have anything to fear from me. I'm just grateful for everything.'

For the last time, I give her a curt nod and then say goodnight. As I turn off the light and go up to my bedroom, I can't help thinking I've done something stupid – as if I've left something behind and it's at risk of being stolen. Have I done the wrong thing tonight?

Just to assure myself, I check on Amy before bed. She's safe and sound.

I hope it stays that way.

Chapter 9
Ruby

I LIE HERE in the night, listening to the creaks and groans in the house. How much of that is the wind outside? How easily would the people inside hear me if I were to sneak around and take a little look around?

Regardless of the answer, it's going to happen.

My eyes adjust to the dark, and I peruse the room. I'm not touching anything – it's way too soon to get caught snooping, but curiosity hits me all the same. There are family photos across the mantelpiece, in which I can make out the figures of two people holding a baby. Lizzie and her husband, Chris.

The rest of the room offers very little in terms of information, so I take it upstairs. There's only one thing I want from this upper floor, so I tread very slowly and carefully to get it. The stairs whine under my weight like it's hurting them. I don't know how – I'm painfully thin.

I'm feeling my way around in the dark up here, completely unaware of the house's layout. Based on what I saw from my car, Amy's bedroom is at the front of the house, but there are two different doors too close together. For all I know, the wrong one could lead right into Lizzie's bedroom. That's pretty much asking to be kicked out and ruin my whole plan.

But if I use the excuse that I'm looking for the bathroom...

I say to hell with it and try the door on the left. The handle lets out a short, sharp squeak, then goes quiet. The door soundlessly opens. Poking my head inside, I use my dying phone to cast a light across the room and explore what's inside.

There she is.

Amy is sleeping like a baby under a pink duvet. Her mouth is open, the pillow spreading her lips apart as she snores lightly. She looks like a little angel – *my* little angel, which makes my heart hurt with this unfamiliar emotion. I can't believe I let her go, but everything will work out just fine. Soon, she will be mine again.

Soon...

SLEEPING on the sofa doesn't sound appealing to most people, but I had the best night's sleep of my life. There were no passing cars to worry about, no murderous cold, and no bumpy suspension every time I turned around. It was just a long, flat cushion in a warm house.

Bliss.

It's Lizzie who gets up first. I've been awake for half an hour now, but when she comes into the living room, I pretend she just woke me up. I'm not sure why. Rubbing my eyes with the heels of my hands, I sit up and yawn like a hippo.

'Morning,' she says before I do.

'All right? Got any coffee?'

'Kettle's boiling as we speak. How did you sleep?'

'Like a log.'

I fold up the duvet and slap the pillow on top of it, then shove it to the end of the sofa. With a big stretch and a popping sound blasting from my joints, I follow Lizzie into the kitchen and stand at her side while she drops instant coffee beans into two mugs.

'What are you guys doing today?' I ask, mostly because whatever they do will ultimately affect my plans. It's been a long time since I've been in this position – chilling out in a house with nothing ahead and no job prospects. What's a girl to do in such a situation?

'I've got a lot of errands to run,' Lizzie says, pouring milk and boiled water into the mugs. 'Some shops to run into, a bank visit, and then I need to stop by a friend's house for a quick catch-up. But I'm not going anywhere until I shower.'

'Fair enough.'

'What about you?'

'No plans.' I shrug.

Before she can reply, Amy comes shuffling into the kitchen in pink Disney pyjamas with a big yawn. Her slippers scuff the tiled floor. Lizzie and I watch her, smiles parting our lips.

'What?' Amy asks.

'Good morning to you, too,' Lizzie says. 'Ruby, would you mind watching her while I shower? Hopefully, I'll be down in time to drink the coffee before it goes cold. You don't need to do anything – just make sure she doesn't run away.'

Of course, I nod. I'd be delighted to watch her, and I once again think about leading Amy out into the car and driving away. Not that I'd get away with it. What I need is a good head start from Lizzie, or I would surely face the wrath of a furious parent.

When we're alone, I take a seat at the kitchen table while Amy uses a chair to climb towards the cupboard. She takes out some cereal, offers me some, and I'm grateful for another chance to be fed. She makes a mess of pouring two bowls of Cheerios, then drowning them in milk. When she's done, she drops it in front of me like a clumsy waitress.

'Thanks, sweetie,' I say.

'You're most welcome.'

Amy sits across from me, and we eat. I shovel it in real fast, only pausing to take sips of my coffee while the shower water runs down the nearby pipes. As soon as I'm finished, I want to probe Amy and learn a little more about who my daughter really is.

'I see you like Disney,' I say, nodding at her pyjamas.

'I like the drawings. I want to draw cartoons like these when I'm older.'

'Good. Which one is your favourite?'

'Mmm.' Amy rubs her chin as she thinks. 'Probably Moana.'

'Can't say I've heard of it. Back in my day, it was all Aladdin and the Lion King.'

'Those are old.'

'Yeah, I guess they are. But so am I.'

'How old *are* you?'

'I'm thirty-six, and let me tell you, that time flies by. It feels like only yesterday I was your age, sitting on the carpet and looking up at a tiny TV screen. They weren't flat back then. We had huge, chunky things with bad screen quality.'

Amy sits up proudly. 'We have a seventy-five-inch OLED.'

'I don't know what that means.'

'I'll show you later.'

'That sounds nice.'

Amy pulls a face like I've just said the weirdest thing she's ever heard. Which is possible, considering she's not got many years behind her and I have no idea what an OLED is. I start to wonder about that when Lizzie returns from her shower in navy jeans and a knitted sweater the colour of blood. Or do they call that red wine?

'You need to go get ready,' she says to Amy. 'Lots to do today.'

'But I want to stay here with Ruby.'

Lizzie glances at me, then quickly looks away. 'You can't. You have group today.'

'Can't Ruby take me?'

'No. Hurry up and put your clothes on.'

'Nuh-uh. No way.'

'Amy—'

I hate to interrupt, but I can't help myself. This is escalating too quickly, and Amy is becoming a little too adamant about what she wants. That's why I raise my hand and offer a suggestion. 'Would it be the worst thing in the world if I took her to that group?'

Amy stares up at her mum, awaiting a response. Lizzie pauses to think, then gives a surrendering sigh. 'Fine. I don't see why not. Just so you know what to expect: it's one big room full of toys and sensory playthings. Lots of parents meet there for coffee while the kids play. It's an hour long, and you're to leave early under no circumstances. I'll drop you both off and pick you both up. I'll even give you some money for a slice of cake.'

'Really?' I beam, not just at the prospect of cake but also at knowing that Lizzie will be God knows where while I'm alone with Amy. It's every opportunity I've been looking for, and it could mean this whole thing will be over with a lot sooner than I hoped. At least then *he* would stop bothering me for updates. Wouldn't that be grand?

'Thank you,' Lizzie says, then tells Amy again to go and get ready.

Amy hops off her seat, takes her bowl to the sink with Cheerios still floating around in it, then bounds off in the direction of the stairs. I'm left alone with Lizzie then, doing nothing but waiting for our little girl to get ready. Lizzie offers me a shower while I wait, and I'm not about to pass on an offer like that.

After all, there's no way of knowing when I'll get another chance.

A SHOWER. A *hot* shower.

When did I get so lucky?

I let the suds wash off me and down the drain in the fanciest shower I ever saw. It's a walk-in cubicle type of thing, with a glass door and soap that comes out of an actual dispenser. I swear to God, these people don't know how to get the best use out of money. If I had even half the wealth

Lizzie and Chris had, I'd be investing in multiple homes to rent out and gain a recurring income. Maybe even treat myself to one of those fancy Mercedes cars.

Now, that's living.

I've barely stepped out when Lizzie calls up to me. We're going to be late, she says. I had no idea the play session was by appointment, but I hurry in getting the same dirty old clothes back on anyway, keeping my hair tied up. I knew there was no time to wash it, at least.

Lizzie and Amy are both waiting for me downstairs, standing by the door with their coats on. I rush to pick mine up off the floor next to the sofa, then make sure I have everything just in case I never return.

Like I said, if I can run away with Amy, then I will.

We all hop into Lizzie's car – Amy in the back seat with me and her other mummy up front. There's not much conversation flowing, mostly because I'm trying not to gag at the summer fruits air freshener swinging back and forth from the rear-view mirror like a pendulum.

You are getting verrrrry sleeeeeepy, I think and chuckle to myself.

Lizzie parks on a busy road, and we all climb out. The 'Play Base' is a small place that looks something like a regular café from the outside. It sits on the end of a row of other establishments: a charity shop, a bank, and a small greengrocer's. We go inside, and I'm immediately surprised by how big it is. It reminds me of Mary Poppins's handbag – looking small outside but plenty of room inside for coat stands and whatnot.

There are kids screaming and playing and having fun with the toys and the sandpit. Most of them are younger than Amy, but it doesn't stop her from running off and heading straight to the corner, where there are cushions and teddies beside a bookcase. She slides one off and gets to reading right away. How did someone like that come out of someone like me?

Lizzie checks in, orders coffee and cake just for me, then gives me a smile. I'm excited at everything that's about to happen, my nerves on edge as I try getting my head around the idea of actually being a mother for once – of finally getting my girl back.

But then that fantasy comes crashing down like a demolished building.

'This lady will be supervising Amy today,' Lizzie says to the beautiful woman behind the counter. 'I'll be picking them up in an hour, so don't let them leave this building, okay?'

As she leans in to whisper something else, I'm trying my best not to reveal how peed off I am. So, Lizzie doesn't trust me. It confuses me that she's still nice to me, considering she thinks I'll run away with her child. Then again, I guess her instincts are correct.

She's right not to trust me.

Because I *will* take Amy at some point.

Chapter 10
Lizzie

IT MIGHT HAVE BEEN the busiest hour of my life. I tried to knock most of the errands out of the way while parked in one spot. Kingswood can be very busy at this time of day, so I didn't waste any minutes by doing it all on foot. When time started to run out, I had to cancel on my friend and rush back to Longwell Green, ready to collect Amy.

I can't believe I left her with Ruby.

Although it could easily be considered one of the dumber things I've ever done, at least I covered my bases by not letting them leave together. They're such a good bunch of people in there, I trust them wholly when it comes to my child. Anyway, Amy seems to like Ruby, so I guess it's not that much of a problem when you get right down to it.

I pull up in the same spot as earlier, parking on the side of the road and mounting the kerb. After quickly checking my hair in the mirror – still blonde and messy – I glance at the time on my phone and relax when I learn there's still five minutes left.

See, it wasn't so bad after all.

After a couple of minutes, I head inside and weave through the crowd of mums putting their kids' coats on. Smiles are exchanged along the way, with the children saying hi and bye to everyone they pass. This kind of energy makes me so happy, I'm excited to see Amy again.

But there's a problem.

A very fucking big one.

The rest of the Base is empty, save for two of the workers cleaning up the mess from the session. Although alarm bells are ringing, I tell myself it might be okay – that Ruby might just be in the bathroom at the back of the room, and maybe she took Amy with her so as not to leave her sight. The problem is the bathroom door opens, and someone else walks out. My knees threaten to give out, sweat beading on my forehead as I realise the truth.

Amy isn't here.

'Where's my daughter?' I ask, marching towards the employees. Their faces turn pale and awkward as they look to each other for the answer. When neither of them has a word to say, I can't help speaking again. 'Tell me she didn't leave. *Please* tell me she didn't leave.'

'I'm so sorry,' the taller one says. 'She must have sneaked right by.'

'You didn't see her go?'

'No, she must have—'

I turn my back on them and run outside. As I slip through the door, I hear the shorter, prettier one say she'll call the police. That works for me because not only do I have to drive around looking for Ruby and my daughter, but there's a nervous lump in my throat that would keep me from saying another word. So I make a beeline for the car with my heart racing, praying to God that I'll find her any minute now – that this is just some misunderstanding.

But somehow, I know it's not.

Amy is gone, and it's all my fault.

. . .

THE MOMENT I'm in my car, my very first thought is to search for Ruby's Mondeo. Keeping an eye on the vehicles on the road, I pull away from my spot with breakneck speed, zip around the corner, and gun it down the residential street with my heart in my throat.

Please, don't be gone.

It's a long, straight road to where I live, and speed bumps stand in my way. It's not too much of a problem – I simply slow down a little, grind my bumper, then continue speeding. Far ahead of me, I see the faint outlines of two people. There's an adult and what seems to be a small child. As I close the gap between us, I see the child's coat is a light pink, and I hate myself for not remembering which coat I put on my daughter this morning. Time will tell, but definitely not fast enough to bring any comfort.

Then I get closer. Closer...

It's not them.

Swearing under my breath and biting back tears, I round the final corner to reach my home. I hold my breath as I slow down, crawling up the street while looking out for a Mondeo. What colour is Ruby's? It was dark outside, and I don't remember it even if I did see.

Relief washes over me when I spot her. She's got a hood up over her scraggy hair, but it's definitely her. If I didn't recognise the tattered coat, the five-year-old girl clutching her hand is a dead giveaway. They're standing beside Ruby's Mondeo and having a conversation. They both look over when I slam on the brakes.

'What the hell do you think you're doing?' I yell at the top of my lungs, parking the car in the only available space and storming towards them. 'Do you have any idea of the worry you've caused? You don't get to do that to me!'

Ruby stands up straight, raises her hands in the air, and backs away. 'I didn't—'

'Save your excuses. Amy, get inside.'

Amy pleads with her eyes. 'But—'

'But nothing. Inside. Now.' As she takes the keys from me and treads her way to the front door, it's taking all of my effort not to slap Ruby across her face. The only thing keeping me from doing it is that Amy is still in sight. And I'm pretty sure Ed is watching.

He usually is.

I take a deep breath, close my eyes, and try to control myself. The rage surging through me is like venom, burning my blood like lava. By the time I've calmed myself – even if just a little – Ruby is looking profusely apologetic.

'Let's talk about this inside,' I say bitterly, then overtake her and head home.

I don't care if she follows or not.

It would probably be best if she didn't.

FUMING, I march inside with Ruby tagging behind me. I knock the door open wider, firmly tell Amy to go upstairs to her room, then stop in the kitchen and wait for the so-called birth mother to catch up. While I stand here trying to figure out what I'll say, I lean my hands on the back of a chair and start anxiously squeezing. Meanwhile, my anger takes a more sinister shape.

'Can I explain myself?' Ruby asks, skulking into the room with her head down. She looks like a school pupil, guilt lurking in her eyes as she's about to get scolded. But it's worse than that – she's lucky I haven't tried hitting someone for the first time in my life. 'If you'll just hear me out, maybe you can forgive me.'

I'm tempted not to, of course. The way I see it, I've been nothing but nice to Ruby, and she's taken advantage of that kindness. But I am curious to discover the true reason for taking my little girl away from the group when I explicitly told her not to leave.

'Speak, and don't lie,' I say, my voice cold as the weather outside.

Ruby comes further into the room, starts to shrug off her coat, then perhaps realises she won't be staying. She pulls it back up her shoulder and leans against the wall, her hands behind her back as if to demonstrate civility.

'Everything was going well at the group,' she says. 'Amy was having a good time, I was making friends with some of the other… I mean, the mums. But then Amy had a bit of an accident in her pants. She told me in confidence and begged me not to tell anyone.'

'That's rubbish,' I snap. 'She always has a change of clothes in the bag.'

'But you took the bag with you.'

I pause long enough to think it through, then begin to consider she might be right. I don't remember taking it with me back into the car, but did I get it out to begin with? Could Ruby be telling the truth about this – about anything?

'So you chose to bring her back here.' I let go of the chair due to fear of breaking it under the mounting pressure. 'What was your plan then, exactly? Neither of you have a key to the house, so that's a wasted effort. Or were you planning to get her in your car?'

Ruby's cavernous mouth drops open. 'I would never—'

'Well, *I* wouldn't know that, would I? You're still a stranger to me.' I exhale slowly, taking control of myself as best I can. 'Then there's the matter of how you managed to leave in the first place. Pretty sneaky of you, wasn't it?'

'They wouldn't let me go while they were watching.'

'And there's a good reason for that!'

'Lizzie...' Ruby lowers her tone and steps forward, only stopping when the kitchen table forces her to. She levels her gaze on me, her deep eyes conveying nothing but hurt. 'You don't trust me, and I completely understand that. I'm also not stupid – I know how it looks. But Amy made me promise I wouldn't tell anyone about her wetting herself. Now, everything you know about me suggests I wasn't raised with no morals, but a promise means everything to me. *Everything*. So, was I desperate to solve the problem and hope to get her in some dry clothes from my car? Sure I was. But *nothing* could make me break that promise.'

The kitchen falls to silence. I'm staring into her eyes and looking to see if there's any hint of truth in all of this. As furious as I am, it's hard to not buy what she's selling. We both know she's had a rough life and certainly wasn't raised well, but if she hangs that desperately on the importance of a promise... does that mean she's really a good person?

'I'll have to check this with Amy,' I tell her. 'If she says you're lying, look out.'

'She won't. I'm really sorry. Truly, I am.'

As she says this, a police car pulls up outside. It suddenly clicks that they're here to look for Amy – the ladies at the group must have called them like they said they would. Not that they're needed any more, but it's assuring to know they come when the occasion calls for it.

'If you want me gone...' Ruby begins.

I know where that train of thought is heading, but I don't even know where to begin processing it.

It's probably not even midday, and my patience has already been run into the ground. Some might call me a fool, but my initial reaction is actually not to evict her from the house. As long as Amy's story checks out, maybe this could be chalked up to a misunderstanding – an error in communication.

Or am I just making excuses for her?

'Let the police in when they knock,' I say, then make my way upstairs to find Amy eavesdropping from the landing. She's sitting on the floor in different trousers from the ones she wore earlier, and the conflicting emotions leave me confused.

'She's telling the truth,' Amy says, a tear brewing in her eyes. 'I'm so sorry.'

I don't know what to say. Nothing hurts me more than seeing my little girl cry, so I drop to my knees and embrace her, stroking her head and telling her it's okay – that she hasn't done anything wrong. She's warm and affectionate, her hair smelling like the strawberry shampoo she loves so much. How can I ever let her go? How can I ever put her at risk?

The front door opens, and a draft blows up the stairs with voices on its breath. I peel away from Amy and give her a half-smile to tell her I'm not angry. I'm upset at the *situation*, but none of this is her fault. It's not even Ruby's fault, really. She may have done the wrong thing, but I truly believe she wanted to help. How can I punish her for that – tossing her out on the street when she needs help now more than ever?

Like I said before, I'm a fool.

Chapter 11
Ruby

SHE ALMOST CAUGHT me on that one.

Almost.

See, most of what I told Lizzie was true: Amy did have an accident, she did make me promise not to tell anyone, and I did sneak her out of the play group to give her some of my old clothes. But there's slightly more to it than that.

For example, nobody saw me pour the water on Amy's leg. Nobody witnessed me drawing attention to it and making her play into my palm. Like I said before, I really did want to change her clothes... and then drive off with my daughter while I had the chance.

But that's our little secret, okay?

The police are on the doorstep now. Lizzie is out there with them, one hand on the door while they share a mumbled conversation. I'm standing nearby, not going anywhere as a show of faith that I can be trusted. I want Lizzie to see me cooperate. I want the *police* to see that.

That's how I earn their trust.

Until my next opportunity.

The phone vibrates against my leg. It irritates me, and not just because of the harsh rattling on my skin. As I take it out and glance at the screen, I see it's *him* again. Of course it is – who else would it be? It's starting to piss me off a little, but it's not like I can do anything about it.

Except hit the reject button, I guess.

The phone is barely back in my pocket when Lizzie finishes up. I hear her saying goodbye to the police and thanking them once again, so I straighten up and try to act normal. I clasp my clammy hands together in my lap, proffering a thin smile as she comes back in.

'So…' she says calmly, almost awkwardly.

There is no eye contact between us. Just fifteen seconds of silence that stretch on for an eternity. It's the kind of peace you'd only hear in a library.

Or a locked room, isolated and in the middle of nowhere. Yeah, that sounds more like it.

It's torture.

'I don't—'

'Let's—'

We both begin together, then hiss with laughter at the same time. We're grinning now, each of us showing true relief in our smiling eyes. I wait for her to speak, letting her choose the course of the conversation because I don't want to force it.

'I'm sorry,' she says. 'I shouldn't have jumped to conclusions like that. That's not to say I fully agree with what you did, but I understand why you did it. I'll give you my number in a second, and that should make it easier for the future.'

All I do is nod, trying to force back my smugness. The fact she wants to give me her number suggests she's willing to let me stick around for longer. It's important I don't push my luck here because I just came so ridiculously close to missing my chance forever. I have to go back to being sweet – to making her think I'm nice.

When really, I'm nasty.

'Swapping numbers sounds good, but do you really trust me after that?'

'I have my reservations, but that can be worked on.'

'Why not just throw me out? You don't owe me anything.'

Lizzie shakes her head. 'You're a human being in need. Despite how uncomfortable things can get, I'm not about to send you back into your car. Although I do think we need to figure something out about Amy. The closer you two get, the less I feel like Mum.'

'You don't have to fear me. That's not who I am. I'm just grateful for the help.'

'I know you are. That's a part of why I like you.'

The awkward silence starts to re-form, so I end it as quickly as possible by taking my phone and asking for her number. As soon as I have it, I quickly dial and let her have mine. Now we're connected, not just by our communicational devices but by our interest in Amy and her future. And with the promise of letting me stay here a while longer, I know I'll win this.

One way or another.

. . .

THE REST of the day makes me feel awkward and, to be totally honest, like I'm being watched. It doesn't look like Lizzie has much to do, so she's baking in the kitchen. The house is filling up with amazing smells, and my stomach makes weird, grumbling noises, even though she made me a sandwich only an hour ago. Even from the living room, where I sit playing with my phone as it charges, all I can think about is stealing one of her pastries.

It's not the only thing I'm helping myself to either.

Not only do I want Amy firmly in my possession, but I've started taking longer looks at the man in the photos around the house. He doesn't look all that special at first – just a regular-looking guy with a particularly good head of hair and a pretty serious look. Chris, his name is. A perfectly normal name for a perfectly normal guy.

At least, it looks that way.

I can't push it too far, though. Lizzie needs to like me, even if she doesn't trust me. I'm not going to get into her good books by asking questions about her husband, so I'm keeping these thoughts (desires?) to myself.

When my phone is charged and I'm sitting

looking at a free game I no longer enjoy, I sigh and put it away. There are trays and dishes clanging about in the kitchen, so I follow the noise and find Lizzie washing some dishes. She looks stressed, her chest heaving up and down as she repeatedly huffs. I don't really want to help her, but this is my chance.

'Why don't you let me give you a hand?' I ask.

'No, it's fine. You just sit back and relax.'

'Absolutely not.'

I roll up my sleeves, then slip between her and the sink. My hands are in the bowl of hot, bubbly water before she gets a chance to protest, and I start scrubbing the bowls and pans she's been using for the cookies that are now sitting on the side. Lizzie thanks me, and I tell her it's the least I can do when she's letting me stay under her roof for free.

'It's not always been this hard,' she confesses, tucking a stray hair over one ear and picking up a dishcloth. She starts drying what I've washed without even looking at me. 'Chris used to work from home, so there was always another pair of hands around. With him gone, the work doubles. You know what I mean?'

'Where has he gone?'

'He works away.' Lizzie tells me her husband goes on long driving trips for work and that she's not sure when to expect him home. 'But I *do* know he's going to freak out if he sees you here without being warned, so I'll try slipping it into the next conversation.'

I nod and finish the dishes, then refuse Lizzie's request for me to go and sit down. She's struggling to keep on top of the chores, she says, and despite the fact that the house looks spotless, I set about cleaning the whole thing for her anyway – furniture polish, vacuum, and window cleaner. I tackle the whole house from top to bottom, which freaks her out at first, but she soon comes around to letting me earn my keep. That's how normal people do it, ain't it?

There's only one room I'm not allowed to clean. I mean, for God's sake, I'm not even allowed to enter it. Amy is in there, colouring her books with the door open. She smiles up at me every time I pass – which is a lot because I love seeing her – and I give her a little wave. When she waves back, it's like the entire world has come to a standstill. My little girl has the most warm, loving eyes that beg me to stay – to not leave no matter how bad things get.

Don't worry, I say in my mind. *I'm not going anywhere.*

As THE DAY turned into evening, enjoying another family dinner – this time, it's pizza ordered in especially because Lizzie wanted to take advantage of having a break today – evening soon turned into night. It took a while for me to get around to the dishes this time, mostly because there were only three plates, so it wasn't worth bothering with. It builds slowly after that, with me and Lizzie adding mugs and glasses, then Amy deciding she wants a snack. I get on it when the pile looks worth filling the sink for, then join Amy and her... *mother* in the living room.

They're not doing anything special. There's something on the TV about a ship that capsized, but Amy has her head buried in a book, and Lizzie is scrolling through her phone. Such a waste, I can't help thinking as I observe this perfect opportunity for family time. They have everything they need for a good night in, and they're spending it looking away from each other. That's not how it should be, should it?

'Why don't we all play a game?' I ask, slumping onto the sofa that's become my bed.

Amy looks up from her book and Lizzie from her phone.

Together: 'What kind of game?'

'Don't you have any board games or anything?'

'Not really.' Lizzie shrugs, and I can tell she's embarrassed to have neglected family time like this. She must be feeling inferior. I would. 'We can probably find something on the internet, but to be honest, it's getting closer to Amy's bedtime.'

'Muuuum.'

'Don't argue. Say goodnight, and off you go. I'll be up in a minute.'

'No.' Amy closes her book and folds her arms. 'I want Ruby to read to me.'

The room falls dead quiet. Lizzie looks at me. I look away. Amy huffs to remind us she's there. We know – we're just both feeling too awkward to say or do anything about it. That is, until Lizzie clears her throat and tries to defuse the situation.

'I don't think Ruby is awake enough to do it,' she says.

'Sorry, Amy,' I say with a shrug. 'Maybe next time?'

Being a child – which is to say she's predictably

unpredictable – Amy scoops up her book, mumbles, 'Goodnight,' and then storms out of the room without looking at either one of us. Lizzie and I exchange a surprised stare that lasts at least ten seconds, and then the next unpredictable thing occurs: we laugh.

Together.

They're full, hearty laughs that make it sound like we're best friends. Maybe in another life, we could have been. Given everything this woman has done for me, I can see us going out together, hitting the cinema or a local bar. We'd have a great laugh, I reckon, even if she does think of herself as a little too above hanging around someone like me.

That's why it surprises me when we chill out together. For the next two hours, we sit and chat about pointless things – opinions on politics or old films – and find we actually have some common ground. I spend a lot of this time wondering if I'll feel guilty when I do what I'm about to do. And not just taking Amy, too – but all the sneaky little things I do in the night.

See, there's nothing on this Earth as vulnerable as a big house in the dead of night. Especially when the man of the house is somewhere out on the road. I think about *the* man – the one who keeps calling and making his demands. He would never let someone like Chris stand in the way of what he wants. To be honest, neither will I.

My goals are very clear, and as soon as Lizzie goes to bed, I'll act on them.

Chapter 12
Lizzie

I AWAKE LYING on my side and watching the dim sunlight creep lazily through the gap between the curtains. It feels a little like summer. Or rather, it would if not for the cold biting my toes. I pull my feet back under the duvet and glance at my watch.

Shit.

I've overslept, which explains the flood of sunlight when I roll out of bed and open the blind. The sounds of muffled talking seep through the floor from downstairs. I can't hear the words, but I recognise the tone and rush downstairs, throwing on yesterday's clothes to intercept any harmful bonding between Ruby and my daughter.

Or am I being too dramatic?

I've had a little time to think about yesterday –

by 'a little', I mean I was up for most of the night – and I've somehow convinced myself it's not all bad. So Ruby took Amy away from the group when I explicitly told her not to... but was that what really happened? There's a memory lodged in my head, but the details are fuzzy. I told the *group leaders* not to let Amy leave. Did I say the same thing to Ruby, or did I forget? It seemed kind of obvious.

But given the circumstances...

Ugh. Whatever. I'm overthinking again, which is exactly the kind of trouble I usually get myself into. Sometimes I want to pummel my own head in with a rock just to stop the thoughts from recycling like a poisoned air con. But there's no time for that.

We're going out for the day.

I don't waste time with make-up or a shower, quickly rushing downstairs to find Amy and Ruby enjoying a book. Amy is sat up straight on the sofa, her envy-inducing posture making her sit up like she's taking a current of electricity. There's a family photo album on her lap, spread open like a bird's wings. Ruby is at her side, chuckling at something. This image should hurt me – seeing Amy with her real mother – but it's kind of nice.

They both look up as I enter the room.

'Going somewhere?' Ruby asks.

'Yes, actually.' I finish pulling my jumper on and go to the window to examine the weather. 'We're going out for the day. I'd invite you with us, but we need a little mother-daughter time. Will you be okay here by yourself?'

Ruby recoils, as if taken by surprise. 'Me? I'll be fine.'

'There's plenty of food in the cupboard.'

'Thanks.'

I look at Amy and give her my mother's recipe – a 'hurry up' raise of the eyebrows that makes her slap the book shut and hop off the sofa, rushing for her coat so we can have that day out we've had planned for so long. I don't blame her for being excited – she really does love the Wild Place. It's a kind of zoo that's full of all her favourite animals. We haven't been there in ages, so she's naturally eager to get a move on.

When we're ready to say goodbye, I give Ruby a list of things that might help her get through the day, then assure her it's okay if she doesn't clean. She laughs as if that's going to stop her, and I'm suddenly grateful she's here. A little bit, anyway.

Outside, in the fresh autumn air, I spot Ed lingering at the end of his drive. He's snooping again, polishing his gate over and over while he waits for us to pass. I know this is going to delay us somewhat, so I whisper to Amy that she should hurry up, zipping up her coat and patting her on the back to encourage a little haste.

But it doesn't get that far. Ed has dropped the charade and is making his way towards us, his wrinkled chin held high as he waves a hand to flag us down. It's really not what I wanted to put up with this morning, but he has information that's worth hearing.

I know this because when he tells me, it almost stops my heart.

'Say that again,' I demand more bluntly than intended. When Ed stares at me with an expression of pure shock in his eyes, I reach out a hand to pat his shoulder, lowering my tone to let him know I'm not hostile. At least, I don't *mean* to be. 'Sorry. But did I hear that right?'

Ed nods, biting his lower lip and taking a short glance back at my house. When he sees it's safe to go ahead and repeat himself, he speaks the quietest I've ever heard him speak. 'I said, whoever that young lady was talking to on your doorstep last night ought to be shot.'

'You mean Ruby? She wasn't speaking with anyone.'

'I assure you she was,' Ed growls. 'Are you calling me a liar?'

'Of course I'm not, but...' I pause long enough to look exactly where he was just looking – at the window where the net curtain is swinging to a stop as if it's just been twitched. We're being watched, and I don't like it. I turn to Amy as I beep the car door unlocked. 'Go and sit in the car, will you?'

'What about you?' she asks, as if it's a lifeboat she doesn't expect me to catch. Her delicate little fingers grope at my coat, which makes me worry she thinks something is wrong.

Who knows? Maybe she's right.

I tell her I'll be along in a minute, then wait until she's out of earshot before I cross my arms and stare Ed dead in the eye. It's not like me to stand off against this guy – or anyone else, for that matter – but when you hear something so alarming, it's hard not to adopt a sinister tone.

'What on God's green earth are you talking about?' I ask, almost hissing the words.

'Exactly what I just said. I would add that he was kicking your flowerpots as they spoke.'

My eyes go straight to my flowerpots. There's not a fern out of place. 'Erm...'

'Okay, so he didn't cause any damage, but that doesn't mean his presence didn't cause concern. This is a nice street, you know, and we don't need any trouble. Do we fully understand each other?'

'No, actually.' I shake my head. 'I don't have a clue what you're talking about. Who was on my property, and why was it such a problem for you? It really seems more like my business rather than yours, don't you think?'

'Don't get smart with me. Just tell me how long the young lady will stay.'

'That's absolutely not your concern. Ed, you need to start making sense.'

'I'm already making sense! How hard can it be to understand?'

My face drops to my palm, where I cradle it as I try to understand what the sudden problem is. Apparently, Ruby had some man on my property last night... could that be right? She's been awfully shady since the moment I met her, but she wouldn't invite people over.

Would she?

'What time was this?' I ask.

'Around midnight.'

'And you were just watching the windows at the stroke of twelve, were you?'

'As a matter of fact, I was.'

'Go on, then, what did this man look like?'

'I don't know.'

'How is that even possible?'

'It was dark, Miss Hughes.'

'Then why did it cause you to worry? And that's *Mrs.* Hughes.'

Ed steps back as I lean towards him, my impatience finally getting the better of me. I never wanted to have to make him feel threatened, but the mystery he's presenting me with is severely lacking in detail. What can I do but become more aggressive?

Or, if I'm smart, change the pace.

'Okay, look.' I unfold my arms and stuff my cold-numbed hands in my pockets. Body language is very telling, and I want him to open up. 'Are you absolutely certain you saw somebody on my doorstep? It's very important that you're sure, because if my guest has been meeting people in the dead of night, then I need to approach her about it. So please, Ed, whatever you do, think about whatever you're going to say next.'

The old man's grey eyebrows go up as if he's

just been splashed with ice-cold water. His face turns a shade of red I've never seen before. It's the colour of blood, and for some reason, that makes me think of Ruby. I chalk it up to ruby being another shade of red.

'Dear heart, if I say there was a man on your doorstep at midnight, you can be sure there *was* a man. I have no reason to lie, no reason to make up tall tales like you're suggesting, and – for the sake of our street's security – I suggest you get to the bottom of who this mystery man is and report back to me.'

Without another word, Ed turns and walks away while whistling some old ABBA song, as if he hasn't just been frustratingly confrontational. As he passes my car, he waves at Amy. She gleefully waves back, her hand swinging around like she's a mental patient, and I find myself wanting to rush to protect her.

But what caused this reaction, I wonder? Is it all the things that have been bothering me lately, all of it surrounding Ruby? Is it the fact there could have been a stranger on our doorstep last night? Or perhaps it's the more obvious and potentially dangerous fact...

That there's a stranger in our home.

There's no way in hell I'll be able to focus on having a good time while such a mystery steals my attention. The secrecy of it all reminds me of a child tugging at my sleeve to beg for my attention. I stand here in the cold, mulling over my options. I could, of course, get in the car and drive away with Amy to continue our day, or I could make her wait in order to find out what's really going on.

The choice seems obvious to me.

I head over to the car just to let Amy know I won't be very long. She complains about the cold, which I fix by starting the engine and turning on the heating while making her promise she won't open the door for anyone except me.

'Mum, I know not to talk to strangers. I'm not three.'

'No, you're five, so do as you're told.'

With that taken care of, I head back to my front door, unlock it, and call to Ruby. She appears in the hallway within seconds, a tall but half-empty glass of water in one hand. There's a lipstick mark on the rim, but she doesn't seem to have noticed. Why would she? She hasn't exactly been good at covering her tracks so far.

'Did you have somebody over last night?' I blurt out, not intending to waste a second on mincing words. I want to add more, in fact, but Ruby's vacant face stares through me, her mouth open and her lower lip drooping.

'No,' she says matter-of-factly. 'Should I have?'

Sucking in a deep breath, I crane my neck to check on my daughter. She seems happy, sitting in the passenger seat with a coat so puffy it looks like it's full of hot air. If she takes off, I wouldn't worry – it's probably safer up in the air than on this street.

I wave Ruby over, then take a step back as she fills the hallway. This way, I can keep an eye on Amy while I get to the bottom of this conundrum. 'Someone saw you out here last night, talking with a man in the dead of night. What do you say to that?'

Again, Ruby looks lost. She shakes her head, then smacks her dry lips together. 'I don't know what you're on about, Lizzie. After you went to bed, I just sat on the sofa and played with my phone for a while. Hate to say it, but your friend sounds like he might be a liar.'

'It's Ed. My neighbour.'

'Oh, then he's definitely a liar.' She seems to gauge my reaction – not amused – then breaks into a half-hearted smile. 'Sorry, but it makes no sense. Who on earth would I have over here? Think about it – even if I knew anyone in this end of Bristol, and I don't, I got too much respect for you to just be inviting them over to your home. Don't you trust me?'

My initial thought is to tell her that, no, I certainly do not trust her. To be totally honest, I'm having a hard time trusting anyone right now. I'm torn between protecting my daughter and trying to do a good thing. There's an obstacle every step of the way. I know I should kick her out, but I assure myself that I can do that at any time, with or without a valid excuse.

I just want to check…

'You wouldn't lie to me, would you?' I ask, locking on to her eyes.

'Nah, Lizzie. You're my friend. Friends don't lie to each other.'

She's half right: friends don't lie to each other. But would she really put me above anything more than an acquaintance? If she does, I don't deserve it. Technically speaking, I'm nothing but the woman who took her child away from her. Sure, it's a lot more complex than that, but that's probably how she sees it.

I shiver again, calm myself with a breath, then nod.

'Okay,' I tell her before walking away.

The whole way back to the car, I can't help thinking I'm doing the dumbest thing ever by trusting her. What she said makes sense – she doesn't know anyone around here. So who *would* she have on my doorstep in the middle of the night?

And why am I having a hard time believing her?

Chapter 13
Ruby

As soon as the door is shut, I move to the window and watch them leave. I want to make sure they're really gone before I go enjoying the space in the house. The car pulls away, and I wave just in case they can see me. It's a small gesture just to let them know I like them.

Which is only half true.

When they're out of sight, I open the door and peer out, hoping to get a minute alone with that piece of crap next door. I knew there was going to be trouble when I came here, but I had no idea it would be this bad. The nosy old bastard is about to ruin everything.

Unless I stop him from being able to, that is.

What was he even doing outside at midnight?

What exactly was it he thought he saw? I must admit, he put me in real trouble by snitching on me like that. All I could do was deny it to Lizzie and pray it worked. It seemed to, didn't it? She believed my lies, at least.

Because I *was* talking to someone on the doorstep last night.

It's not like she'll find out who either. Just like every other secret in my godawful life, I'm keeping it close to my chest until I have no other choice but to drop the bombshell – to hit them with a truth I'm not sure they can handle. In such an event that Lizzie is on her knees and begging me for mercy, I'd tell her there's only one thing I want in exchange for her life.

Amy.

It's not a bad day, to tell you the truth. I wish I was spending it with Amy, but that doesn't mean I can't enjoy myself. I've got this massive house with its empty halls and multiple bedrooms. The TV in the living room is so big it looks more like a billboard. And the best thing yet? The fridge is full of food. At least it is until I start eating from it.

There's no shame in taking this stuff. Lizzie

said I was more than welcome to eat whatever I liked. Now, I know most people are just being polite when they say that, but I've been on the streets for so long I don't hesitate for a single second before tucking into all the good stuff: cheese, sliced ham, some leftover sausages, and let's just say more than one chocolate bar. My stomach hurts by the time I'm done eating, but it's not like I have to go anywhere. Today, I can relax completely, and I do just that.

Until I get more text messages.

They basically say the same thing they always say: that I should check in with him and give him a full update on the situation. I've got to confess he scares me at the best of times, but not enough to make me call him. What would I tell him, anyway? That I'm still working on it? That there has been no progress and I need more time?

Yeah, like that's going to happen.

I plug the charger back into my phone and get up with a huff. The house is too quiet. The only sounds are from the hideous grandfather clock by the front door. I head back to the window and let out a soft sigh of boredom. When will they come back, I wonder? Soon, hopefully.

Or... I could use this opportunity.

The upstairs bedrooms call to me in silence. I look up the stairs, consider that I could get caught doing this if I'm not careful, then decide I'll do it anyway. I'm already ascending the stairs while I slide my nail-polished hands up the bannister, feeling like an old Victorian widow stalking around the house. Maybe not a widow – maybe a ghost.

The first room I find has a double bed and some décor that looks disgustingly rich. The headboard is rich mahogany, and the sheets are silk. I'm assaulted by an overbearing flowery scent as I go inside, wondering just how long I can stand to be in this room.

Long enough to find what I want, hopefully.

I drop to my knees beside the bed and pull out the drawer. There's nothing of worth in here – just a vibrator and some old blankets. I rummage through, shoving aside small, empty boxes for Lizzie's iPhone and headphones, but there's nothing interesting.

Carefully putting everything back as it was, I slide the drawer shut and try the walk-in wardrobe. These people must be rich because this space is bigger than the bedroom I had as a kid. The lights come on automatically, almost blinding me as it highlights countless pairs of shoes and handbags.

They're all Prada and the like. Too rich for my blood, which only makes me resent Lizzie more.

After all, it's one more thing she has that I don't.

I shut the door, take one last look around the room, then decide to leave it alone. I'm wasting time looking at Lizzie's stuff when I could be exploring Amy's bedroom. I head over there at once, walking the long stretch of hallway and wondering if I could snatch her in the night. Unless Amy screamed at the top of her lungs, Lizzie might not even wake up.

Nah, it's not worth the risk. I only get one shot at this.

I have to do it right.

Amy's bedroom is all pink, just like any little girl's ought to be. There are half-peeled animal stickers on the walls that haven't stood the test of time, and there's a row of perfectly aligned books sitting on a shelf by the door. I walk around, soaking in the atmosphere and wishing I'd been there to help set up this room. I ain't got no money, but if I did, then I'd have used it to give her the room of her dreams.

I pick up a stuffed teddy from the bed and examine it, noticing this one has been given more care than the others. It has grey fluff and a love heart in the middle that says, 'I LOVE YOU', which makes me feel a little sick. Did Lizzie get this for her? Is it Amy's favourite?

I'll never truly know.

Enduring the great weight of misery, I sit on the bed and realise just how tired I am. It wouldn't kill me to sleep here for a little while, enjoying the comfort of the mattress despite it only being a single bed. The duvet is soft and smells of my daughter, so I hold it close to my nose and try not to cry.

She's not *my* daughter. Not any more.

Or should I say not *yet*?

Time rolls by, and I hear some murmurs outside. I ease out of bed, then go to the window to find Ed Warner standing in the street. There are two women in front of him, but their body language says they want to get away. A short, pitying laugh escapes my mouth, and I stand around to watch the interaction.

What a sad, desperate old man he is. It sickens me to think he's been keeping tabs on me, reporting my late-night rendezvous to Lizzie. I have every right to go down there and give him a piece of my mind. As soon as I start thinking like that, it's hard to let go of the thought. Ed almost cost me everything, throwing a spanner in the works just to create some drama.

Well, someone has to set him straight.

And that's exactly what I intend to do.

When I get down the stairs and head outside to give him a piece of my mind, the two women he was talking to have made their escape and are walking away while rolling their eyes. One of them looks at me, taps her friend's hand, and then the friend looks. I'm not uncomfortable about this – as a prostitute, I've had a lifetime of people pointing at me. Some of them laugh, some of them sneer, but none of them matter.

As soon as they pass, I put the latch down on the door to keep it from shutting, then storm down the drive with my arms folded across my chest. Ed hears me scuffing my feet, turns to see me, then scowls as if I've already had a go at him.

He's in for a shock.

'Think you can go around causing trouble for me?' I ask, walking until my face is almost touching his. I let him feel my hot breath, like it's an indicator of my wrath. 'You think it's okay to poke your nose in other people's business, old man?'

Ed steps back, his jowls shaking along with his head. That gross wattle reminds me of a turkey, and then his face reddens, and he looks more like an old pig. 'You leave me alone, young lady. The last thing any of us need is for you to become irate.'

'Irate? You haven't even *seen* irate yet. What the hell did you tell Lizzie?'

'I told her exactly what I saw.'

'Which is?'

'That you were talking to a gentleman on the doorstep at night.'

My chest is heaving up and down as I try to control my temper. A woman passes us, a small boy closely at her side as she pushes her other child in a pram. They all stare, clearly sensing the drama, but I keep my mouth shut until they're out of range. Anyway, some good has come from all this: he saw the man at the door but didn't see his face.

Really, I dodged a bullet there.

'Is there something else, or may I continue with my day?' Ed asks sarcastically.

'No, you may not. I want to know exactly what your problem is.'

'Is it not obvious? I'm trying to protect the peace on our street.'

'Am I a threat to that somehow?'

'Well, it's not as though you're welcome here.'

'Excuse me?'

My voice booms so loud that one of the front doors opens nearby, and an elderly woman pretends to fidget with her knocker while listening. Two curtains twitch in windows across the street, and suddenly, we have an audience. I don't mind – everyone I meet thinks I'm worthless and pathetic. Why should Longwell Green be any different?

Ed shakes his head, that loose skin flapping around like a dog's ear again. I try to hide my disgust, but his attitude is already making me snarl. There's a look in his eye now – like he's finally realised that his generation can't just go around acting however they want, leaning on the privilege of making people respect their elders. But in the real world, or at least in modern times, people can treat older folk however they want.

And I want to be nasty.

'Let me make something clear,' I spit through my teeth, stepping forward and getting right in his face once again. This time, he doesn't step back – he just stands there as his cheeks turn from lily-white to bloody red. 'You're not going to talk shit about me ever again. If you do – or even if I *think* you do – I'm going to come back here, and it won't be so pleasant.'

'Huh.' Ed grunts. 'Are you threatening me, young lady?'

'What do you think?' I lean in so our noses are touching, making sure he's the only one to hear me. The words leave my lips in a whisper just loud enough for him. Just enough to inflict the fear I so desperately want to cause.

'Try me, you old fool, and I'll snap your goddamn neck.'

Sadly, there's no time to see the look on his face. But I don't need to. His silence tells me everything I need to know: that not only does he regret ever having opened his mouth, but that he won't be doing it again any time soon.

Not if he knows what's good for him.

Chapter 14
Before...

AS THE WEEKS WENT BY, my clients started to drop off one by one. See, I was starting to show, and a lot of men didn't like that. Not only were they grossed out by the idea of life growing inside me, but I think some of them started to panic it might be theirs.

I felt the same way.

There was no way of telling who the real dad was. It was easy enough to narrow it down to eight, but the harder I thought about it, the less sense it made. It wasn't like I fell pregnant on that particular day, so I had to consider the clients from the days before and after. That's when more possibilities entered the fray, and suddenly, there were over twenty potential fathers. More than anyone would want to know, for sure.

I thought about just choosing the one who was most well off – the one who would give me hush money to ensure I didn't tell his wife. But then he'd want me to get an abortion, or it could backfire, and he could hurt me somehow. I tried not to be surprised by how badly a desperate man could behave, but I had to consider everything.

Even money.

I was pretty desperate. My income was starting to take a dive, and soon, I'd have two mouths to feed. How was a woman like me supposed to keep working while there was a baby growing in my belly? It felt weird to see it in the mirror and even weirder to say it aloud. How terrifyingly odd would it feel to actually give birth to this thing, much less raise it?

No, the baby had to go. Maybe not by termination – I don't believe in killing kids, even if it would be to everyone's benefit – but there was never any chance of this child having a good life. Not with me as their mother, at any rate. So, no matter how much I wanted to keep it, there was only one horrible way this was going to end.

I had to carry out the pregnancy, then give the baby away.

Chapter 15
Lizzie

I WOULD NEVER SAY this out loud, but it's sort of refreshing for Amy to fall asleep. I love her far more than words can say, but moments like these – where she's sitting in the back seat of my car, head rolled to one side as the seat belt supports her cheek and it looks like she's just been knocked unconscious by Rocky Balboa – are pure relief.

It's been a good day and easy to forget the crap that's been happening lately. The centre of Bristol has so much fun to offer a five-year-old girl, and clearly, it's enough to incapacitate one, too. The quiet drive home is just the cherry on the cake.

Around ten minutes from home, we hit a speed bump. The car jumps. Amy stirs. I sink into a small flashback of when my father used to call speed bumps 'sleeping policemen', and it makes me miss him. I wonder what he'd make of this whole situation. I'm willing to bet he'd make me stand up straight and dig my heels in, showing Ruby absolutely no mercy or compassion of any kind. But that's Roger Wilsher for you – stern but fair. He'd also ridicule her name until she sounded like nothing more than a silly comic book character.

Ruby Wishes.

It even makes *me* chuckle.

I try to control the vehicle's speed for the next sleeping policeman, but it's a big one. A quick glance in the mirror shows me the back of Amy's throat as she yawns and stretches, her eyes slowly blinking open while she tries to examine her surroundings.

'Have we reached our destination?' she asks, as if she's some rich lady and I'm just her limo driver. She huffs out another yawn, rubs her eyes, then meets mine in the mirror. 'Mum? Did you hear me? I asked if we've—'

'We're not there yet, no.'

'How much further?'

'Five or ten minutes.'

'Will Ruby be there?'

'Probably.'

She doesn't say any more, but she doesn't need to. The thin smile on her face is bursting with the innocence of her youth. She doesn't understand the situation, and she wouldn't have a mature opinion on the matter even if she did. I have to keep reminding myself that, every time she seems to prefer Ruby over me, it's not personal. I mean, farts still make her laugh, for crying out loud. She's not exactly of sound, full-formed mind, is she?

The rest of the journey is spent by Amy telling me about her new career move. It changes every week. Last week, she wanted to be a court judge (which explains why she's been forcing good speech of late). This week, it was a cartoonist, and just now, she's decided she'll move on to being one of those people who trains dolphins to dance. One thought leads to another, and then we're finally home, my head pounding with the onslaught of silly questions she keeps hurling my way: if animals could talk, what would be the rudest? What body part would I want double of? What was the best moment of my life?

'That one's easy,' I tell her as I park on our street. 'The moment you first laughed.'

Amy giggles proudly, then hops out of the car. I follow suit, grabbing her bag from the back seat and suddenly feeling the full effect of the morning's exhaustion. When I move to hand it to her, she's staring dumbly towards our house, her tiny mouth open in a little O. Amy is full of strange expressions, so I think nothing of it and prop her backpack onto her shoulders.

It's not until I turn that I see what she sees. My heart starts racing, my hands instantly clammy as my brain tries to make sense of what my eyes are seeing. I'm trying to process the word, but excitement and confusion are fighting for attention in my groggy mind. Then, Amy beats me to it, screaming out the word before running towards her hero.

'Dad!'

It's like I've been hit by a speeding truck. Like I'm frozen in time after my soul leaves my body. Amy is already speeding up our pathway towards the front door, where her father is standing with a backpack resting against his leg. He kicks it to one side when he sees his daughter, rushes forward, then drops to his knees to embrace her. She barrels into him with such force that he tumbles backwards, laughing even as he hits the concrete. Amy chuckles on top of him, smothering his five o'clock shadow with kisses while I struggle out of my trance.

'Chris?' I say breathlessly, finally catching up as they clamber to their feet.

The front door is ajar as if he was just in the process of arriving home after all these weeks. Amy lugs his massive backpack into her little twig arms, then rushes inside to help like the world's smallest porter. Meanwhile, my husband of five years is standing there with a smug grin on his face, still looking as youthful as the day I met him. He was twenty-seven back then (looked twenty-two), and it's like he hasn't aged a day. With the exception of a few silver hairs and a wrinkle or two, but that's a given.

'Hey, Wifey,' he says like a stoic hero returning from war.

I rush forward without a word and attack him with an enormous hug. It's less aggressive than Amy's in impact alone, but it's infinitely fiercer with how intensely I hold him. His arms wrap around me, squeezing me tight just like I've been dreaming of for all these weeks. Finally, a warm tear rolls down my cheek. I never realise how much I miss him until he comes home. I always cry. It's almost ritualistic in nature.

'When did you get back?' I ask, taking his hand and leading him inside, where I tear off his coat and put it on the hook beside the door. 'How was work? Where did you have to go? Will it be a while before you have to go back on the road?'

Chris laughs and pecks me on the cheek. 'One question at a time, but let me get in the door first, okay? I'd kill for a coffee and a few minutes with my family.'

I can't stop grinning – I feel like an idiot teenager obsessed with her crush. I know that's not normal and that relationships grow old and stale more easily than music and films suggest, but you can't blame me for loving a man I barely see any more.

We make our way into the kitchen, where Amy has dragged a chair across to the kettle and has started preparing two mugs and a glass for herself. It's already full of orange juice, and she's dropping teabags into the mugs while the kettle starts to roar.

That's when I remember we're a person short.

'Have you seen Ruby?' I ask Amy as quietly as possible.

'In the living room.'

I've no idea how to explain this situation to Chris – the last time we spoke about it, he flew off the handle for letting a stranger into our home. Despite how badly I tried to explain that she's not just some random stranger off the street, he wasn't happy about how close I let Ruby to her daughter.

Our daughter, I remind myself again.

Before he finds out the hard way, I touch Chris's arm with a guilty smile and encourage him to the far end of the kitchen. The happy grin drops from his face when he detects the seriousness in mine. There's no delicate way of putting this, and Ruby could walk in here at any minute, so I have to terminate this joyous reunion with all the grace of a sledgehammer.

'We have a guest,' I say, smacking my cracking lips with my tongue. 'I'm so sorry, I went against what you advised and invited Ruby into our home. Now, before you say anything, I know it was wrong, and I'll be the one to tell her to leave. I just want you to know that it was my compassion that made me do it. No matter how hard I tried to get rid of her, it was—'

'I know.'

My brain freezes up, my mind along with it. 'You... what?'

Chris's smile widens, as if he has some deep secret I'm not privy to. He lets me suffer for a moment, as if punishing me for my godawful actions these past few days, then softens and explains. 'I called by the other night when I had one last delivery to make. I didn't manage to make it inside because a random woman intercepted me at the doorway.'

'That's... Ruby?' I'm still stunned.

'Yep. Although I was shocked at first, I found it kind of endearing that she was asking me loads of questions about who I am and what business I had around here. It's like she was trying to protect you guys, which made me trust your judgement a little bit.'

I can't believe what I'm hearing. It's not just that he already knew about Ruby – and seems okay with it – but that he was here the other night and I didn't even know about it?

The puzzle pieces fall into place. Suddenly, I feel terrible.

'Any chance this was around midnight?' I ask.

'How do you know?'

I shake my head ashamedly. So Ruby *did* meet someone late at night – my own husband. Ed didn't recognise him because it was dark, and she didn't give up the secret, even when it jeopardised her home. The only thing I can't figure out is... 'Why?'

'Why what?' Chris's face is one of creased-up bafflement.

'Why didn't you tell me you were here?'

'Because I wasn't technically home yet. The company was making me drive right through, so I needed another day. But I had to make sure you were all okay, so I stopped by. Ruby confirmed you were fine, then I made her promise not to tell that I'd been by. I didn't want you all to get excited. It's not a secret how much you love surprises.'

This certainly is one, I think as I settle into silence. After the incident with Amy at the play group, this is the second time Ruby has put herself out to keep a secret for my family, and I've been confrontational with her both times. It makes me feel bad that, after everything, I'm still treating her like the enemy – as if she doesn't deserve to be here.

But there is one thing she does deserve: an apology.

And she's going to get one right now.

I FIND Ruby in the living room, sitting on the sofa with a look on her face that says she's pleased with herself. She's picking at her nails, giving me the side-eye as if unsure whether I'll be excited or offended by the lie she told. The lie she *needed* to tell.

'So, now you know,' she says without looking up.

I suck in a deep breath and let it out with a sigh, then go and sit beside her. The sofa cushion weakens under me, and it's like sitting on a cloud. Ruby smells like cheap perfume – the kind kids wear and is basically sugar water – but it weirdly suits her. Besides, it's better than how she smelled when I first met her. The scent I could only describe as 'dusty'.

'I'm sorry for losing my temper with you,' I say. 'You being here has made me a little uneasy, and when Ed said you had a visitor, I couldn't help but fear the worst. It's not much of an excuse, but that's the truthful reason. I get it if you're upset with me.'

Ruby finally lowers her hands and twists her neck to look at me. Her head rotates like an owl's. She gawks at me with those big, beady eyes. 'I ain't upset with you. Why wouldn't you ask questions about the people on your property?'

'I had to be sure.'

'Course you did.'

'So... I'm forgiven?'

'It ain't my place to forgive you. You did nothing wrong.'

My hand reaches out to touch hers, and my lips curve into a smile. Ruby reciprocates, her jagged teeth on show while this short moment of bonding builds between us. It's funny – I never expected to end up liking this woman, but as I get up and make my way back to the kitchen, I can't help thinking I might feel a bit sad when the time comes for her to leave. Not that I have any idea when that is. With Chris home and him suddenly understanding why Ruby came here in the first place, there's no reason to kick her back onto the street and upset the rhythm. Anyway, Amy really likes her.

So I guess she can stay.

Chapter 16
Ruby

I'm no idiot.

When Lizzie asked me to stay, I somehow knew it wouldn't last forever, but it's obviously going to come to an end sometime soon. Which means my time is limited. I'll have to snatch Amy at the next possible opportunity.

But it's easier said than done. Even before Chris came home, it was a nightmare to get a moment alone with her. Now that they're reunited as one big, happy family unit, who even knows when my next chance will present itself?

If this evening is anything to go by, the next few days will be everything an orphan ever dreamed of. We're sitting at the dinner table, two large pizza boxes flopped open from the greasy moisture. Our stomachs are full, but despite the discomfort and the stuffed exhales blowing around the table, there isn't an unhappy face in the house.

'There's still two more slices,' Lizzie says with a lazy sweeping gesture.

Chris is the only one who bothers to move, rushing forward to scoop them onto his plate. He only pauses long enough to look everyone in the eye, confirming he's not about to deprive them. But it's my gaze he holds for a few moments longer.

I wonder if...

'So, Ruby.' He slumps back and prepares to take a bite. 'You're a working girl, huh?'

'Chris,' Lizzie hisses.

I shake my head. 'It's fine. I *am* a working girl.'

'Do you get pensions for that kind of thing?'

A short laugh escapes me. I can't tell if he was trying to be funny, but there's no way that question could be taken seriously. My chuckle extends into a stream of humoured huffing, and then I finally break into laughter. Lizzie erupts next, and then Chris is laughing at the awkwardness around the table. Tears spill from my eyes. As I smear them away, I see Amy just long enough to recognise the lost expression on her face.

'What's a working girl?' she asks.

'It's someone who works every day,' I say, my laugh simmering down.

'Like Dad?'

'I'm not a girl,' Chris says. 'But it's an outdated expression. Don't use it.'

'*You* used it.'

'And I regret it.' He checks his watch. 'Bedtime, young lady.'

There's very little protest. Amy works her way around the table, kissing her mum and then her dad. When she gets to me, I expect she'll tone it down and go for a hug. But that's what shocks me the most – her lips find my cheek, and she softly plants a kiss there before heading up to bed. I touch my cheek and wonder if she'll still want to kiss me in the future.

When I've taken her away from the life she knows.

THINGS GET a little easier when Amy is in bed. For starters, our conversation is aided a little by a couple of bottles of wine that Lizzie has pulled from her stock of favourites, and it goes right to my head. I don't drink much, mostly because it usually ends in violence, sex, or violent sex. But I can't see any risk of that happening tonight – it's just the three of us.

Another thing that keeps us mellow is the topic of conversation. We've moved far away from my past as a sex worker, circling the standard themes such as Chris's work, how the weather has been lately, how they're going to handle Christmas, and the like. To tell the truth, I'm starting to feel a little excluded from the conversation. Lizzie must have sensed this because her hand is soon on mine as she offers to pour more wine.

'Maybe just a small glass,' I say, then watch as she tops me right up. If I didn't know any better, I'd say she's trying to get me drunk. Though I don't know why – nothing good can come of it. I try to imagine what it might be like if I just give in and drink all I want.

Like I said, only bad things would happen.

As Lizzie heads outside to dispose of the empty bottles, Chris and I are stuck alone together. It's not our first time speaking one on one, but now his gaze is holding mine. Physically speaking, he's way too good for Lizzie.

'It worked,' he says, sitting forward.

'What did?'

'The surprise. She had no idea I was going to be here, but there's a problem.'

'What's that?'

'I worry about getting you into trouble.'

I've no idea what to say to that. Sure, Lizzie was ready to evict me after finding out I was talking to a man on her doorstep. I don't even blame her for feeling so threatened. After all, she had a right to feel like that. Her family is definitely in trouble when I'm around.

'She's forgiven me' is all I can think to say.

'And thank God she did. It's a pleasure to have you here.'

'Did you miss it?'

'Miss what?'

I gesture around the room at the beautiful kitchen with polished marble and white tiles. The back door is open, a slither of wind creeping in while Lizzie clatters bottles out back. Chris seems to get my meaning because he picks his teeth and nods.

'There's plenty of thinking time on the road. All the good thoughts pop in. All the bad ones, too. But mostly, I get to think about what my family are up to. Until my mind wanders, that is. After that, I've just got one thing on my mind.'

There it is. Some stirring in my loins. A tingle of fresh excitement I haven't felt in years. Chris's eyes find mine again, pinning me in place as if daring me to read between the lines. My heart flutters at those little hazel pools.

'What's on your mind, Chris?' I sit forward and let him peek down my top.

'Well...' He scratches his stubbly cheek. 'Sometimes it gets so lonely I need—'

The back door shuts. Lizzie shivers audibly, making a show of how cold it is outside. Chris breaks eye contact with me, and I start sipping on the wine again. It's red – not my favourite because it makes my head flush with heat. Not that I'd be cold without it.

Thoughts of some alone time with Chris are keeping me more than warm enough.

We're sitting on the floor in the living room when it happens. The Monopoly board is spread between us, and coasters rock on the carpet whenever Lizzie encourages us to use one. I take a sip and then keep it in my hand, using it as a prop to cover my sneer when she asks.

'What exactly is your plan now, Ruby?'

The room feels silent in spite of the gentle piano music emanating from the TV speakers. Chris glances at her and then looks back at me, his slightly skewed vision trained on my eyes but occasionally sneaking a look at my chest. Lizzie hasn't dared to look in my direction yet, which helps me hide how stunned I am by her sudden, confusing question.

'My... plan?' I say, lifting the glass to my mouth. 'For what?'

'As much as I like to be generous, you can't stay here forever. So let's imagine you're leaving tomorrow. Tell me, what is the very first thing you would do?'

I take a sip and let the fruity red sit in my mouth before I swallow. 'Am I leaving tomorrow?'

'No. Not at all.' Lizzie sits up, puts down her Monopoly money, then rests a hand on Chris's shoulder. Chris says nothing while she smiles. 'I just mean hypothetically. You must have an idea of where you'll go, what you'll do?'

'I've not really thought about it,' I confess.

'Not at all?'

'Nope.'

'Come on, don't be shy.'

'Well, I wanted to come and meet Amy. Now

that I have, it's probably more about how long I'm *allowed* to stay. I don't want to take advantage of your generosity, but it's really nice to be able to spend some time with her.'

'I won't tear you away from her at a second's notice.'

'You won't?'

'If all is well, you'll get some notice before we have to say goodbye.'

The most I can offer is a grateful smile, aimed at both her and Chris. They then turn to each other with lovers' looks, peck each other on the lips, then go back to counting their money. I'm about to do the same when my phone vibrates against my leg.

'Excuse me,' I say, taking a look, then putting it away when I see his name again. Lizzie's curious eyes flick up at me, but she doesn't ask who tried to call me. Which is just as well because I don't want to lie to her any more than I have to.

The wine goes down a little too easily from there on. Chris kicks both our bums with his... well, *monopoly* over the market. Lizzie grows more and more frustrated, biting her nails as she desperately tries to make bargains with money she doesn't have. It's a landslide that I bow out of and watch until she finally gives up and climbs uneasily to her feet.

'I'm going to bed,' she says.

'Do not pass GO,' Chris insists. 'Don't you dare collect two hundy.'

I try not to laugh. Lizzie pulls a sarcastic ha-ha face and stumbles past. She stops beside me, tilts over slightly, then quietly whispers something in my ear with her wine-soaked breath gusting down my neck.

'Make sure he cleans up the game.'

I laugh a little too falsely, then say goodnight. I actually have every intention of helping Chris clean up the mess, but the phone is going off like fireworks in my pocket again. I excuse myself and rush to the hallway, saying goodnight to Lizzie one last time before reading the message on my phone.

Update. Right now.

I'm getting tired of his constant demands but even more of his tone. It's hard to keep the exact energy of a message pure while only using text, but everything I know about this guy says he's not in a bad mood. I can sort of picture him now, sitting in a massive room that's too expensive to be anything more than a visual statement. That smug, no-nonsense demeanour of his and the brash abruptness in which he talks. There's a certain danger in him – there always has been, and I sometimes forget just how much trouble I can be in if he's displeased.

That's the only reason I leave a voice message.

'I'm getting closer. Any day now.'

I leave it at that because I don't want to be heard. Lizzie could be lingering at the top of the stairs, and Chris might have stopped what he's doing to check in on me. It's not exactly flattering that they don't trust me, but like I've said a hundred times, I'm not to be trusted.

Take tonight, for example. We've had a lovely time as a family, and the hosts have worked very hard to make me feel like I'm a part of it. They bought me food, have put a roof over my head, and I'm still fortunate enough to be allowed near little Amy. Most people would be over the moon and eternally grateful for the help.

But me? I'm a different breed of nasty.

That's why I'm about to go and screw Chris in the living room.

Chapter 17
Lizzie

THE NEXT MORNING, I wake up to Chris's snoring. That's the one thing I don't miss when he's travelling – I usually get to sleep solidly until it's time to get up. But right now, my husband sounds like a blocked pipe. Weirdly, he usually only does that when he's really exhausted, like when he's been working flat out or we were up all night having sex.

Neither of which have happened.

Regardless of his sleepy grunting, I roll away from Pumbaa and throw on yesterday's clothes before heading downstairs. There's so much to do today, but Amy's schedule is clear, so I let her sleep in. Down in the living room, it's kind of pleasant to see Ruby has folded up her duvet and opened all the curtains. The room is bright and airy as it should be, and she's sitting on the sofa while scrolling through her phone.

'Morning,' she says when she spots me, the Bristolian in her voice twisting the word harshly: *moor-nen*. At least the smile is warm, even if it is a little crooked. 'What are you doing today? I was thinking of a family meal.'

'Sorry,' I say with a *tsk* sound. 'My plate is full. Excuse the pun.'

'Oh no. How come?'

'I just have a long list of errands.'

'Then how about I cook us all breakfast?'

A smile reaches my lips. 'Really? You'd do that?'

'It's the least I can do in exchange for all your generosity.'

Ruby gets up and heads for the kitchen, leaving me wondering why she's suddenly putting in a ton of effort. I don't want to overthink it, so I focus on waking up Amy and Chris. They both moan at me like teenagers when I open their curtains and let sunlight flood their rooms, but they're both downstairs with smiles on their faces when they find the bacon sizzling in the kitchen and fresh orange juice poured into glasses. I don't mind either – it's nice to be on the receiving end of a cooked meal for once.

'Ruby cooks better than you,' Amy tells me as she stuffs a sausage into her mouth.

'Hey, that ain't very nice,' Ruby says from across the table.

'Sorry.'

Amy lowers her chin, clearly disappointed that her backwards compliment didn't earn her any friends. I'm not sure how I feel about Ruby disciplining my child, but I let it slide because it's otherwise a nice morning. When Chris looks over at me, I start to wonder if he's thinking the same thing. I offer him an awkward smile and start to move on.

Then I see it.

It's unclear if I'm just being paranoid or if this is a giant waving red flag, but I'm almost certain he gave Ruby a wink. Maybe he really did and I'm just overthinking it. That can't be the case... can it?

A sudden sickening feeling unsettles my stomach and murders my appetite. Chris hasn't winked at me like that in years. In fact, I can't recall a single time he ever did. Is something going on between these two, or is my imagination doing me wrong?

'Lizzie?' he says, breaking me from my deep, depressing thoughts. 'You okay?'

'I'm fine,' I tell him with a fake smile. 'But we do need to talk.'

There it is again. A communication between the two of them using nothing but their eyes. Chris's are full of guilt, whereas Ruby just shrugs like they're having a private conversation, and then she goes back to biting off another slice of toast. There's definitely something strange going on between them, and I'm determined to find out what.

But the real question is... how?

It gets a little too much for me. It's hard to explain exactly why, but I shoot to my feet and dart out of the door as fast as possible. There's a weird aura around the house right now, almost as if it isn't mine or no longer will be. That feeling makes me uneasy. No, not uneasy.

Sick.

A chair screeches against the floor tiles in the kitchen. Footsteps pad after me. With the way I'm feeling, I don't want anyone knowing what's going on, so I head upstairs and into my bedroom, where I shut the door and fight back the urge to cry.

What on earth is going on with me?

I barely make it to the bed before the door clicks open. There goes my intention to curl up and cry – to let out whatever bizarre emotions have just come over me. On the other hand, in comes Chris with a furrowed brow and the caring expression of the dutiful man I married.

'What's the matter?' he asks as if he has no idea. Not that I blame him.

Even *I* don't know.

I settle for a shake of the head because it feels like my voice will croak if I dare to speak. When Chris shuts the door, I flop down onto my pillow and let him come to me, sitting at my side and lightly caressing my leg in the same way he always has. This has always been my comfortable spot – right here beside the man I love.

'Everything feels... a little off,' I confess.

'With me?'

'No. Not even with Ruby, but with you two together.'

Now there's a new look coming from him. Something I haven't seen before, and it resembles genuine confusion. Maybe I should take that as a sign that this is all in my head, but one thing it does clear up is that I know what upset me in the first place.

I was feeling paranoid about the two of them.

'What are you thinking?' he asks bluntly.

'Is there something going on between you and Ruby?'

'Ruby?' His head snaps back with shock. 'The hooker in our kitchen?'

'You know she's more than just a hooker.'

'But that doesn't change the fact she's a sex worker. Besides, I'm very happily married.' His hand comes off my leg and finds its way to my face, where he tucks wandering hairs over my ear. His hand is warm, his touch warmer. 'You know I could never do anything behind your back. Especially with someone like that.'

I don't know what he means by 'someone like that' – perhaps the prostitute, or it could even be how rough around the edges she is – but it's comforting to hear. I lean my cheek into his palm and close my eyes, then suck in a steadying breath.

'Sorry,' I say. 'Maybe it's the stress getting to me.'

'Well then, why don't I help you out?'

'What do you suggest?'

'How about I take Amy out for the day and tick a couple of errands off the list. You can go do your thing, then we could both be back by the evening.

Then, I could take you out for a nice family dinner tonight. Just you, me, and Amy.'

'No Ruby?'

'No Ruby.'

'You promise?'

'Cross my legs and hope to fart.'

A short chuckle breaks the discomfort, and we're back to normal. Chris leans in and plants a firm kiss on my cheek, then double-checks I'm okay and heads back downstairs to check on the girls. As he's making sure they're safe, I take an extra couple of minutes to let the threat of tears subside, enjoying the soft cushioning on our bed.

'You're being ridiculous,' I mutter to myself as I replay the downstairs events in my head. There may or may not have been a wink between them, but even if there was, who cares? Chris and I have known each other for a long time, and not once has he ever given me a single reason not to trust him fully.

Ruby, on the other hand...

No, I can't let myself think like that.

Only bad things will come of it.

CHRIS DELIVERS, and I don't mean for his job.

The restaurant is a British franchise that I won't name because they prefer to identify as American Italian. It makes no difference to me – we've been eating there for years and have become very friendly with the waiters and waitresses. I should hope so, too, with everything my husband tips them. They don't always deserve it, but he gets kind of generous. Especially when he's had some beers with his dinner, which he won't be doing tonight because he's playing taxi.

We both order the steak because I don't like to cook it at home, but Amy – who is extremely over-dressed in her navy blue dress with frills on the long sleeves – orders a chicken burger and some potato wedges. Ever since it was put in front of us, she's barely touched any of it. I think I know why, too.

She's saving herself for dessert.

'I've eaten so many burgers on the road,' Chris says, prepping a slice of medium-rare meat onto his fork, 'that I was starting to forget what real food tastes like.'

'Burgers *are* real food,' Amy protests.

'Not if you get them from fast-food chains.'

'What's a fast-food restaurant when it's at home?'

I scoff a short laugh as I spread peppercorn sauce all over my fries, then glance around at the near-empty restaurant. It's usually busier at this time of night, but I don't mind – we got our food pretty quickly, and we can actually hear each other talk. Although when I see a familiar figure lurking in the doorway, all the background noise fizzles out.

'Ruby!' Amy yells, beating me to the punch, then leaps out of her seat and scurries towards our guest like an energetic little elf. She moves so fast that I can't tell her to sit because she's gone before I even swallow my food.

Chris looks over at the door, then back at me. I shrug, as clueless as he is at this point. I was starting to think we would actually get five minutes alone as a family, and now this morning's feelings have all come shooting back up like vomit.

'Sorry,' Ruby says, her voice stern and her face serious. 'I'm not staying.'

You got that right, I think, then say, 'Is everything okay?'

'Actually... no.'

'What's up?'

'Can I talk to you alone for a minute?'

Now it's my turn to look at Chris, who shrugs

back as if we've reversed roles. I dust the sauce off my lips with the napkin and then stand. By now, Ruby is shaking Amy off her hip as calmly and coolly as possible. I tell Amy to sit down, then follow our guest outside to the shocking wind that sweeps across the dark car park.

'This had better be good,' I say, growing braver with my anger.

'That depends on your definition of good.'

'Spill the beans, then.'

Ruby takes a step back and looks through the window. I follow her gaze to see my family still at the table. A young, skinny waitress is at their side, scribbling something onto her notepad. A dessert order is my guess, but it's not important.

'It's about Chris,' Ruby says with a breath.

'What about him?'

'I don't know how to tell you this...'

My heartbeat has almost doubled, drumming in my ears like the gallop of a furious stampede. Anxiety and impatience have bred to form an ugly baby that looks incredibly pissed off. When will all this drama end?

When Ruby leaves, probably.

'Just say it,' I demand a little too snappishly.

'Please don't hate me for this...' Ruby is looking anywhere but at me.

'I'm starting to. Blurt it out.'

'You'll think I'm lying.'

'Try me.'

The wind picks up and sweeps hair in her face. Both our teeth chatter, and I cross my arms against my chest. Although I'm not sure if it's because of the cold or because I'm feeling defensive. Maybe a bit of both. Ruby, however, takes a dramatic breath. Then, just as easily as she came into our lives, she destroys my world in a single sentence.

'Chris came on to me last night.'

'He *what*?'

'It's true. He—'

'No, no. Shut up a minute.' My finger points straight up, instructing her to wait while I fight off a burst of tears. I should have known this had happened. Everything I suspected at the breakfast table was exactly right. Chris *did* wink at her, and now I know why. There *was* something going on between them, and all I can hear is my husband lying to me, telling me he's happy with me, promising he would never do such a thing.

'What happened?' I ask, feeling my stomach unsettle once again.

'I was just on the sofa after you went to bed, and he offered me money for sex.'

'No. That can't… I mean, he wouldn't…'

Ruby steps forward and takes my hands in hers. They're cold as ice, which my tears feel like they're quickly turning into as they distort my vision. I don't even have the balls to question whether she could be lying because there's only one person who can give me the truth.

And he's sitting right inside.

Chapter 18
Ruby

I'm not completely proud of myself.

I wasn't exactly telling the truth either.

But what even is the truth? Not that Chris tried touching me up or that he offered me a generous donation of cash in exchange for the good stuff. No, all of that is actually better than what really happened, but this is far more convenient.

For me, that is.

Lizzie's face has drained to sheet white. Even with the limited light from the nearby car park lamp, I can see the blood rush from her cheeks. She looks like a ghost, staring in at her family and probably asking herself what to do. She reminds me a bit of that Christmas Carol film where Michael

Caine (depending on which version, I suppose) looks in at his life from an alternative future. And just like Scrooge, she's probably trying to figure out her absence.

'Promise me you're telling the truth,' she says, her voice void of all emotion. 'Tell me just one time that what you said happened *did* actually happen, and I'll never question it again.'

There's no kind way to say it, so I just rest a hand on her shoulder and pretend not to notice when she shivers. I lower my voice to something calm and reasonable, kind of like when I'm settling the nerves of a client.

Then I lean in and whisper the lie.

'It happened,' I tell her. 'I promise with everything I have.'

If she ever had a chance of hiding her tears, that chance is well out of here. Lizzie shrugs my hand off her shoulder and makes a weird noise as her body convulses and the crying intensifies. Should I comfort her or smile? Make a joke of it or tell her the truth?

Nah, any of that would only make it worse.

So I do all there is to do – I stand back and make a path between her and the restaurant's front door. While she continues to bawl like a baby, I fish through my handbag for a pack of tissues and hold them out to her. It's not that much of a shock when she snatches them from me, dabs her eyes, then breezes past me while shaking her head.

The damage is done. That much is clear as day.

I move to the window and watch her strut across the restaurant, her long, flowing cardigan trailing behind her like a humble wedding dress. Amy doesn't look up from her ice cream – *good girl, you just enjoy these people for the last time* – but Chris stands to attention and moves to embrace his wife with the same hands that touched me last night.

That were *all* over me while we fucked like bunnies.

The window feels like a cinema, and I'm the only viewer. The film is about a woman who finds out her husband is a rat, and meanwhile, someone is plotting to take their daughter away in the very foreseeable future. 'How?' is one question for the audience, but the more fitting question is 'why?', and the viewers will only have to watch for the answer.

When I'm sure my confession has caused enough trouble, I begin the long walk home in the cold. Can I call it that now: home? Something tells me I won't be welcome much longer, but that's fine. I don't need much time. All I really need is to process this bizarre feeling – an interesting cocktail of pride and shame. I've wrecked a family, and I'm about to do worse.

Like I said before...

I'm not *completely* proud of myself.

It ain't just a long walk home, but it's a cold one. I'm thinking about getting a taxi with the money I took from Lizzie's purse, but I'm going to save it for something better. Maybe I'll get Amy something nice to win her over. The idea that she could end up preferring me over the people who raised her does tickle my funny bone.

I can't feel my cheeks or hands when I get back. The spare key Lizzie gave me seems to dance around the key ring, evading the grip from my stiff, numb fingers. While they jingle around and my patience cuts in half, I hear the sound of a familiar voice over the nearby wall.

'You're still here?' Ed says.

I don't even look at the old fart – don't need to because I've already put him in his place. He knows I'm going to hurt him if he keeps interfering with my business, so I simply clear my throat as I finally get a grasp on the key.

'I'm here until I need to be. What's it to you?'

'Like I said, you're not welcome around here.'

'Like *I* said, I'll snap your goddamn neck.'

All I hear next is an embarrassed grunt. It's like he knows I'm not bluffing but doesn't want to walk away without at least an ounce of his pride intact. Makes no difference to me – I'll follow through on my promise if he keeps this crap up.

I finally get inside and shut the door on the wind. The whistling dies as if music has just suddenly stopped. I'm alone in the Hughes's house once again, with only the hallway lit up to greet me like a stunningly bright red carpet. I dump my handbag on the side and then make my way through the house, turning on the lights as I go. God knows how long I've got, but there *is* time to snoop again, and I *am* going to use it.

This time, I start in Amy's room, going through her clothes and smelling them like some creepy weirdo with a crush. This isn't a crush though – it's true love, the way only a mother can love her child. But the clothes don't smell like her. They don't carry any cherished memories simply because we don't have any. Instead, they smell like lemon or whatever fruity washing powder they were cleaned with. It's pleasant, but it's not right.

I take one quick look out the window to make sure the family aren't coming home, then stand there for a moment to check my phone. My contact hasn't called me ever since my last update, but I know I'm running out of time. I can feel it in my muscles, the way they all tighten whenever the thought crosses my mind.

Stealing Amy is time sensitive, after all.

Stuffing the phone back into my pocket, I cross the hall and open the laundry cupboard, where I know Chris put his suitcase upon returning from his work trip. It's easy to find and even easier to open. His clothes are still in there, along with a couple of phone numbers from girls I can only imagine he got from some bars along the way. I quickly put them in my pocket to use against him later, just in case I need to rock the boat a little more. It brings a smile to my face, almost as much as when I seduced him last night.

I won't lie – it was good sex.

A sound travels up the stairs and hits me like a gunshot. I can tell the front door is open as the wind chases me down the hall. They're home, I realise as I quickly put everything back where it was and then close the cupboard door. There's nothing for me to do but head downstairs and face the music – to get wrapped up in the drama I just caused.

And maybe, just maybe, cause a little more.

THEY START SCREAMING before I even reach the landing that overlooks the hall. I haven't prepared an excuse as to why I was up here in the first place, but I can probably say I'm heading to the bathroom and pretend I didn't know there's a downstairs one. There are lots of curse words being hurled around, and Amy comes pounding up the stairs into my arms. I hug her tight, holding my baby girl close to my chest while I stroke her hair and hush her.

This is how it always should have been.

And how it will be again... sort of.

As magical as it is to stay locked in this moment, it's torn away from us by the furious call of my host. Not Lizzie, but Chris. His voice bellows up the stairs, calling my name as if an angry god is summoning me. I set Amy down and tell her to go to her room.

'He's ever so upset with you,' she says, then kisses me on the cheek and runs off.

I take a deep breath to calm my nerves, then make my way downstairs in time to see Lizzie close the door. The chill lingers, so I wrap my arms around myself and go into the kitchen as per Lizzie's instructions. There, I find Chris, leaning against the back of the island stool, gripping it so hard his knuckles have turned white. The creases on his forehead speak of unrivalled fury, which I completely understand.

'Did you tell my wife I tried paying you for sex?' he snaps, getting right to the point.

I look to Lizzie, who has taken her spot in the doorway, mirroring my self-hug. My chest heaves up and down as I sigh. It's immediately clear that I need to either own it or back down entirely. I already know which path to walk.

'Of course I did.' My head snaps back towards Chris. 'Because it's the truth.'

'You know as well as I do that this is complete bullshit!'

'Then what really happened, Chris?'

I challenge him with my eyes because the truth is so much worse. He lingers in that painful state, unable to answer it honestly. The truth does implicate me, too, but it would surely cost him his marriage. That's a risk I'm willing to take.

'Tell Lizzie what really happened,' he says.

Is he bluffing?

There's enough time for me to consider my options. Nobody is going anywhere, and the happy couple are hanging on my every word. Should I just spit out the fact that we had sex, or should I stick to my original story to see how it plays out?

The latter sounds great to me.

I turn to Lizzie and meet her gaze. 'Whatever he told you, it's complete rubbish. I came out tonight to tell you what he did because I thought you deserved to know. You're a good person, Lizzie. Unlike your husband, you're so kind and honest. You deserve better.'

'Who the hell do you think you are?' Chris screams, swiping a glass off the island. It hits the wall and rains into a hundred crystal shards. Lizzie jumps out of her skin, but I'm too busy feeling through my pocket for the newly found evidence of his betrayal.

'Here,' I say, handing her the phone numbers. 'Your husband left these lying around, and he should really be more careful. I believe he got these while on the road. Probably hasn't even decided which order he wants to call them in.'

The kitchen goes dead silent. You could cut the tension with a knife.

Or cut *someone*.

Lizzie holds out the paper – three sheets, each with a different female name on them. I can hear Chris stammering, desperately trying to conjure an excuse for his infidelity. I've got him hook, line, and sinker. There's nothing he can say to stop the tears from wetting his wife's eyes, so we all just stand there in the painful silence.

Until...

'Ruby, can you go out for a walk or something?' Lizzie scrunches the papers into a ball, then hurls it across the kitchen. She doesn't look at me because her deadly gaze is fixed on Chris, who still hasn't thought of what to say. 'I don't want you around for this.'

All I can do is nod while I head back to the hallway and grab my coat. My back is to them both before I start grinning because I've put him right where I want him. All I did was lay out the bait, and now they're going to have the biggest argument of their lives. Meanwhile, I get to take a nice, quiet stroll around Longwell Green and wonder if Chris will even be there by the time I get back. Judging by how Lizzie looked when she saw those phone numbers, he doesn't stand a chance of holding his marriage together much longer.

And with him out of the way, taking Amy will be much, much easier.

Chapter 19
Lizzie

Do you have any idea what it's like trying to keep your daughter safe when the entire family is falling apart? I've got Ruby taking Amy away without my permission, Chris trying to sleep with other women, and Ed Warner in my ear every five seconds. I'm up to my eyeballs in drama, and I'm getting pretty sick of it.

Last night ended as badly as it began, too. After Ruby left, we had a long 'conversation' – which is a delicate way of saying I could have hurled a lamp at his face and not felt bad about it – during which he insisted he hadn't done anything wrong.

'Those numbers stayed in my suitcase for a reason!' he insisted.

'What, so you could call them later on?' I countered.

'I was never going to call them.'

'Then why not just throw them away?'

Chris paused, and that told me everything I needed to know: he's a cheater, a liar, and neither of those things are going to change. At the end of the day, I couldn't trust him to go back on the road again. What would stop him from inviting a woman into his truck?

No, he had to go. I told him as much, and he went with little more to say. I couldn't figure out if that was because he knew he'd been cornered or because he wanted to make a display of how reasonable a man he was. If it was the latter, I wasn't fooled.

Needless to say, I had a sleepless night. Likely because I didn't bother going to bed until Ruby got home. She offered me some of my own tissues from the bathroom, which made me want to scream at her. Thankfully, I remained somewhat level-headed. It wasn't her fault all this was happening. Sure, she added to the drama, but it wasn't her fault.

Just to avoid having to talk to her, I then went up to bed and endured the tornado of thoughts that wreaked havoc on my mind. Hours later, the sun comes up, and I feel even worse for wear. Not only do I have all this trauma to sift through, but I have to look after Amy for the day. Unless I want to entrust her to Ruby.

So... I have to look after Amy for the day.

All I can think to do is take her to the park. She doesn't ask why I'm less talkative than usual, but she waits until I'm putting her coat on before presenting me with a small origami flower. I freeze when I see it, wondering where on earth such a perfect craft came from.

'What's this?' I ask.

'A rose, you silly goose,' she says in that posh little voice of hers. She sounds like a Victorian lady on helium. 'I heard you and Father shouting last night, so I thought you might be sad. I learned how to make it from a book you gave me at Christmas. Do you like it? It might even be my calling. Perhaps I should pursue a career in origami...'

Honestly, I could cry right now. Not the same kind of crying I did all night – those were tears of sadness and frustration – but to see how my beautiful daughter was so kind-hearted and warm completely knocks me over. What a wonderful young woman she's becoming.

'Thank you,' I say and take it with a genuine smile, then put it on the side for later.

We continue to dress up for the cold. Amy dons her gloves, and Ruby passes just long enough to say goodbye. Before we know it, we're out of the door and coming face to face with Ed. My heart almost stops at the sight of him because he has that same look of concern he normally has, only with slightly more apprehension. He tries to peer over my shoulder through the door, but I pull it shut to stop him.

'Can I help you?' I ask snidely.

'No, but *I* can help *you*.'

'So says every gypsy woman I ever met. Goodbye, Ed.'

I take Amy's gloved hand and try to squeeze past him, but then his hand rockets out and seizes my arm. I inhale a cold, sharp breath and spin around as if to hit him. But his features soften, and suddenly, I see real worry in his eyes.

'I'm not going to make a show of it,' he says in a much calmer tone while the wind ruffles his white hair, 'but I just happened to be passing last night and saw that young lady of yours rummaging through your things. Through the window, of course.'

I glare down at Amy for a split second before I realise she's not the young lady he's referring to. Ed is talking about Ruby – a woman my age. I have a sudden image in my head of her stirring the trouble at the restaurant and then heading home to snoop through my things. Would she really do that? Would she really take advantage of my generosity by invading my personal space while my marriage is falling apart?

There's little need to distrust Ed. He may be nosy and a damn sight more invasive than any man his age should be, but I trust him enough to believe it when he tells me what he saw. After all, he was right about a man being on my doorstep the other night, wasn't he? Even though it was Chris, he had no trouble telling me the truth of his findings.

Suddenly, I fear leaving Ruby alone in the house. As if I have a choice any more. Just like everything else in my life, I have absolutely zero control. I'm spinning too many plates, and it's only a matter of time before every one of them falls and shatters.

As if this morning wasn't going badly enough, my husband comes strolling up the drive. I'll bet he's curious about the new aggravation caused by Ed, but that doesn't give him the right to approach me when I specifically asked for time to think.

The only reason I don't go back inside is because Ruby is there – Chris will follow, and then I'll be stuck in a house with the pair of them, and Amy won't get to go out for the day. I don't want her to see any of this anyway, so I excuse myself from Ed, we go our separate ways, and then I trudge down the gravel drive towards the gate.

'Good morning,' Chris says moodily. 'Can we talk?'

'Absolutely not.'

I breeze right past him, still holding Amy's hand and wishing she would walk a little faster. Just enough to get away from my lying, cheating husband. Admittedly, I don't have proof that he *has* cheated, but I'm convinced he wanted to. That's bad enough.

'Mother.' Amy digs her heels in, forcing me to stop. 'Can you two not come to a resolution? It appears this rivalry between the two of you could easily be overcome by simple conviction.'

A breath escapes me, half humoured, half embarrassed that a five-year-old has played the logic card and won the entire game. My eyes flick up towards Chris, who's grinning down at his daughter with something between a laugh and a sneer.

'*The Watchtower*,' he says.

'What?' I ask.

'That quote is from a film called *The Watchtower*. I've seen it a thousand times and know every line. But she skewed it – it recommends communication, not conviction.' He bends over and musses his daughter's hair, making her giggle. It even makes me smile a little.

Just a little.

'Why are you here?' I ask bluntly, killing the mood. Although the others don't seem too bothered by it. They're still smirking at each other, at least until Chris puts his tongue out at her and then turns his attention on me.

'I thought maybe we could talk. A little "conviction" goes a long way.'

'Now isn't a good time.'

'Why, what's up?'

I look over his shoulder at the front door and wonder if Ruby is inside watching. If Chris dares to contradict what she told me last night, she might even come bursting out to cause a scene. Well, that's not something I want. Not while Amy's here, and certainly not while the wind is turning my nipples to stone.

'Just... not now,' I tell him firmly.

'Why though? Can't we just talk this through like adults?'

'No. Later, perhaps.'

'When later?'

'Later!'

Amy pulls away as I raise my voice, and suddenly, I feel like my mother. She would shout all the time, which terrified me when it caught me off guard. Now, my heart is burning with regret, so I kneel in front of her and cup her chin between my thumb and forefinger. She pulls away from my cold touch, but still. 'I'm so sorry, sweetheart. It didn't mean to come out like that. Can you forgive me?'

Amy looks between me and Chris. There's knowledge in her eyes, like she knows she's in a position of power. I'd bet any money she's about to use this to her advantage, suggesting I talk to her father as an apology.

That's why it comes as such a shock when she just nods.

My heart is broken. I've done something wrong, and I'll continue to do it because I just can't face having this conversation with Chris right now. There's enough going on in my mess of a head, and my suddenly troubled marriage will just have to wait.

I say as much, and nobody is happy – not Chris, not Amy.

And certainly not me.

It's dark when I get back. Amy has fallen asleep in the back seat of my car, and I'm luckily able to carry her up the stairs and into bed without waking her. I stand in the darkness of her bedroom for a few minutes, watching my little angel sleep. I'm killing time, of course – I saw Chris sitting with Ruby in the living room, and I'm dreading facing them.

At least I had some time to think. Hearing that Ruby has been snooping through our house suddenly bumped Chris off the top spot in my list of problems. Being walked all over by your own husband is one thing, but I won't take it from a complete stranger.

I already know what I'm going to say when I go downstairs and into the living room. Chris has moved to the opposite sofa, away from Ruby, who is looking at me while wringing her hands. Maybe something was going on when I was out, but it's not my problem any more.

'Did you look through our things?' I ask her directly.

A moment's hesitation and a side glance at my husband. 'Of course not.'

'The problem is I don't believe you.' I suck in a breath and wheeze it out with a sigh, then go and rest on the arm of the sofa beside her. 'Ruby, I've been nothing but good to you since the moment you arrived, but things are getting out of hand.'

'I'm sorry, I didn't mean to—'

'It's okay, I'm not angry about it. I'm trying not to be, anyway. But my daughter lives here, my family is falling apart, and it's no longer suitable for you to stay here. I'm going to leave a couple of hundred on the side for you to take when you're done packing up your things, just to help you along your way.'

Chris is stirring at my side. I honestly don't know if he's relieved or angry about this. But he doesn't say anything either way, so I turn to him and let him know exactly what I've been thinking throughout this long and tedious day.

'You need to leave, too,' I tell him, watching his

face drop. 'At least for a day or two so I can get my head straight. Between the two of you, there's been enough toxic behaviour to last a lifetime, and I need to finally put my foot down for the sake of my mental health as well as my daughter's. If you can't respect that, we have bigger problems.'

The room falls deathly silent. Nobody moves. Nobody speaks. Not until Ruby stands up to start packing the folded pile of clothes from the corner of the room, stroppily stuffing them into her bag. When she's done, she lingers long enough to ask one last question.

'Can I at least say goodbye to Amy?'

'She's sleeping.'

'I won't wake her.'

'She's sleeping.'

'But if I'm quiet—'

'I said she's sleeping, Ruby!' I'm on my feet in the bat of an eye, gritting my teeth and pointing my finger directly in her face. 'Forget about the money I was going to give you, okay? You've shown me nothing but disrespect since the moment you showed up. Just leave, and don't make this harder than it has to be. You too, Chris.'

They both take their time heading for the door, but at least they're doing it. Here's the problem:

I'm not a strong person, and I'm definitely not a bad person, so it takes all of my willpower to watch them sulkily head out the door. I want to call them back – to tell them they don't have to spend the night out in the cold – but it's no longer a viable option. I have to protect my family, even if that means sending my husband away for a little time.

All I want is some time to think.

Is that too much to ask?

Chapter 20
Ruby

WELL, I didn't see that coming. Neither did Chris, judging by the look he gave me right before we walked to the end of the driveway side by side but in deadly silence. When we reach the end, I don't hang about before turning right and heading to my car.

Before I'm stopped dead in my tracks.

'That wasn't your brightest move,' he says.

I spin around, the bag strap grinding a hole in my shoulder before I dump it at my feet and try to control myself. It's hard to say exactly what I feel for Chris. Technically, he hasn't done anything wrong, but he's also a speed bump in my plan to abduct Amy. Or to *reclaim* Amy. It's all a matter of perspective, ain't it?

'All I did was tell her you came on to me,' I say.

'Which we both know isn't true.'

'The details aren't important.'

'Ruby, you lied to my wife. You made me out to be the bad guy when the truth is that I was minding my own business until you came and straddled me like a goddamn horse! But did you tell her any of that? No, of course you didn't. You twisted and manipulated the story in whichever way possible, and now I may lose my whole family because of you.'

There's nothing to say, so I keep my mouth shut and think back to that night. He's right – I did make the first move, and then we had the best thirty minutes of sex a woman could ask for. I wonder if Lizzie knows how good she's got it. Or *had* it, depending on whether they stay together after all of this.

I can't see it happening.

'Are you even listening to me?' he spits.

'Well, whoever came on to who ain't important.'

'Not important?' Chris shakes his fist like a furious caricature, then points back at his house, where the net curtain twitches with Lizzie's shadow behind it. She's watching, listening, so I need to play this very carefully. 'You destroyed my family!'

'No, you did that when you tried to pay me for sex.'

'But that didn't happen!'

'Deny it all you like, but look where your actions got you.'

'Ruby...' He stops long enough to sigh. I've seen this look before. He's trying to control himself – to make sure he doesn't make a wrong move, say the wrong thing, or perhaps even lash out physically if he's that type of guy. 'Just... do us all a favour and get out of our lives forever. It was all good until you came along.'

Without another word, he spins on his heel and walks down the street with nothing but a jacket and a bad temper. I stand around for a moment, wondering what I'm supposed to do with this situation. It's tempting to head back to the house and beg for somewhere to stay because the prospect of spending another night in that freezing, stinking car is daunting. But I need to be so careful and not rock the boat any further. It will ruin my plan.

Speaking of plans, what can I even do now? I didn't foresee being thrown out of the house. Chris is officially out of the way, so at least there's no strong leader in the family to stop Amy from going missing, but it's easy to remember I'm on the outside now. I'll have to strip down my plan and rebuild it with whatever pieces are left.

The only one sure thing?

This has just become urgent.

I *will* get my daughter back.

I WOULDN'T GO SO FAR as to say Longwell Green feels like home, but some of the faces are becoming really familiar. There are dog walkers that pass with a smile, as if we've met and talked, but I can't recall how I know them. When I hang around in Starbucks just for a little warmth (I don't buy anything because I'm not exactly well off), a lot of heads turn my way. I can't figure out if it's because I look like a working girl or if it's because they've seen me before and want to say hello. Regardless, I smile fake as hell and sit down to watch the cars come and go in the car park outside. The sun beams through the window as if to trick me, telling me it's lovely and warm outside, but we all know that's not true.

It's bloody freezing.

I'm just starting to wonder what to do with my life when a plate lands in front of me. A second later, a large mug of steaming coffee is put down beside it, the glorious smell of fresh caffeine working its way right through me. I crane my neck to see a man in his fifties, with overly long sideburns beneath a full head of grey hair. Crow's feet sit at his eyes, which he somehow manages to smile with. He looks familiar, but God knows how.

'You look like you could do with a pick-me-up,' he says, pointing at the coffee and red velvet cake he just put down. 'A gift, from me to you.'

'Sorry,' I say, all flustered and confused. 'Do I know you?'

'Not really, but we've passed a couple of times. At the Chapel café and at the Halloween fair. You probably saw right through me, but I can tell when someone's having a hard time, and I couldn't resist doing my part to help a stranger.'

I don't really know what's happening. Is he trying to get into my knickers, or is this truly just a selfless act of kindness? I quickly spot the wedding ring on his left hand, but in my experience, all that does is make him look more desperate for physical attention.

'You're married,' I say.

'Yes, my wife is over there.'

As he takes a seat and hikes a thumb over his shoulder, I strain to look at the small counter, where an older lady is pouring milk and sugar into two mugs on a tray. It's not just surprising that this stranger is being so nice, but it's heart-warming. Men are rarely nice to me without wanting something in return. Thankfully, this isn't one of those instances.

'Thank you,' I say thoughtfully.

'You're very welcome. So, how do you know Lizzie Hughes?'

That catches my attention as I wrap my hands around the hot mug and eyeball the cake. 'How do you know I know Lizzie?'

'You were together at the Halloween fair.'

'Of course. She's a friend.'

'Good for you. She's a nice person.'

That may be true, but it doesn't mean I'm not going to go through with it. I came to Longwell Green to get one thing – no, not a thing but a person – and I'm absolutely not leaving without her. It doesn't matter how nice her adoptive mother is.

'I did wonder,' the man says, picking at his yellowed fingernails, 'if you were her new babysitter. So it came as a bit of a surprise when my Jess accepted a shift at short notice.'

'What are you talking about?'

'For tomorrow night? Lizzie asked my granddaughter if she could babysit young Amy while she goes off to some clay modelling class or whatever it is she does.' There's an awkward pause. 'Oh, you must be going with her.'

I nod, not in agreement but just to shut him up for a minute while I figure this out. So, Lizzie is out of the house tomorrow. There must be no sign of Chris, otherwise he'd be sitting at home with Amy. So this babysitter...

'How old is your granddaughter?' I ask, hoping for more information.

'Just sixteen. It's so hard for them to make money these days. With the way the world is, it's a wonder anyone can afford to live. When I was her age...'

The old man's voice trails into the background, disregarded while I try not to laugh at how lucky I've become. What are the odds that I'd bump into the one talkative man who could give me a golden opportunity? So the house will be empty tomorrow night, save for the weak and pathetic sixteen-year-old assigned to watch over Amy. Teenagers are barely adults themselves, for crying out loud. Getting past her will be no problem at all. Even if I have to do it by physical means. It won't matter if I leave marks or bruises or even a trashed house in my wake because nobody will be around to stop me while I leave that house with Amy.

I drag the plate towards me and pinch off a bit of cake. The cream touches my tongue and tastes incredible. I savour it for a moment, still grinning, then swallow it and turn back to my new companion – the man whose friendliness has just cost Lizzie a daughter.

'So,' I say, wiping crumbs off my lip. 'Tell me more about tomorrow night.'

I'm not moving my car. There's nothing anyone can do to make me, although I have to admit I'd rather not get caught. Night has come early once again – that happens in this cold, miserable time of year – and I'm parked a little further up the road. Just enough to be less conspicuous, but not so far that I can't see their house any more. Some people might call this spying.

I just think it's opportunistic.

While I wait under the blanket of darkness and

far away from the street light, Lizzie and Amy come back from whatever they've done and make their way outside. Lizzie takes a peek at where my car used to be, sees it's now been replaced by a neighbour's car, then follows Amy inside and doesn't come out again. At least, that's probably how it will stay for tonight.

That's fine, I think. Tomorrow night will come.

With nowhere else to go and nothing else to do, I get comfortable in the back seat of my Mondeo. When everyone is asleep, I'll consider running the engine so I can blast the heating for a while, but for now, I have got to be discreet. So I snuggle into my pile of clothes and check my phone. There's just enough battery to send a text to *him*, and it's best to do it before he starts hassling me. Which wouldn't take long, for sure.

You won't have to wait much longer. Tomorrow night is my chance.

I send it, then immediately suffer panic. What if something goes wrong? What if I can't take Amy away and it gets me in a whole lot of trouble? He was already losing his patience, and now I've made a promise I'm not even sure I can keep.

Hardly a minute goes by before my screen lights up. There's a reply.

It had better be.

My mouth has gone dry. The phone shakes in my wavering hands. It could be the icy-cold that's working through the fabric of my multiple layers of clothing, but I know real fear when I feel it, and this is it. I can't disappoint – I won't, no matter what.

As soon as I put down my phone, my attention is drawn to a light that blinks on outside the car. I sit up, the suspension rocking beneath me while I squint at the light and try to see what it is. When I find it, the irritation in me leaves no room for surprise.

Ed Warner is in his doorway, a torch in his hand that's pointed right at my car. I don't know if he's trying to unsettle me or if he simply wants to check that I'm in the car, but I don't like the way he stands there staring at me. That miserable old bastard has caused enough problems for me already, and I'd do anything to leave his body in a ditch. Unfortunately, one wrong move will ruin everything. I have to be careful, so I just wait.

It takes a long couple of minutes before he turns off the torch and goes back inside. Should I expect Lizzie to come around any minute now, demanding that I leave the area? Will the police come around and tell me to move? I hate to let Amy's house out of my sight, but it just might be the best thing to do. I shouldn't draw attention to myself. Not when I've come so far after all this time.

Not when I'm this close.

Chapter 21
Lizzie

The morning starts sharply and abruptly. I awake on the sofa with my hair matted all over my face, my eyes slowly fluttering open and my dry mouth tasting like a dog's bum. I roll my tongue around inside to produce some moisture as I sit up and listen for what I thought I heard.

Seconds later, it comes again. The rapid knocking on the front door followed by two rings of the doorbell. I'm starting to think about disconnecting. While I climb up unsteadily and regret last night's emergency bottle of red wine, I glance at the clock and see it's only six. No wonder it's still dark in here – the day hasn't even begun.

Groggily, I open the door to find my worst

nightmare standing there, his long, tattered old brown coat draped around him and looking like it hasn't been washed since 1992. The grey hair whips around his head in the violent early morning wind. Ed shakes his head from side to side, as if disapproving of having waited on the doorstep for so long.

'It's six in the morning,' I groan at him. 'What are you doing?'

'Sorry to disturb you – I really am – but there's something you should know.'

A half-yawn, half-sigh widens my mouth like a cave. I cover it, but barely. I'm not awake enough to use manners properly, and maybe that's evident in my tone as I bitterly ask the only question that needs answering. 'Why are you here, Ed?'

'It's about that woman.'

I roll my eyes. 'Ruby?'

'She's causing trouble.'

'Not this again...'

'She only just left.'

Whatever initially made me want to shut the door in his face is now gone. My hand has already found its way to the lock. I'm prepared to swing, but I don't like the worried tone of his voice. Nor am I comfortable with what he just said. 'Just now?'

'About ten minutes ago.'

'But I checked the street last night.'

'The whole length?' Ed takes my silence as an answer and then comes up a step, so close that I can smell the Irish coffee on his breath. At least until he pivots and points over the fence at his own house. 'See that empty spot right there? She was parked there all night. Now, unless she was trying to hide from you, why would she move the car?'

'Perhaps because I told her to leave.'

'For all the good it did.'

'Did you speak to her?'

'No, but I did go out there with my torch to confirm it was her.'

'When was this?'

'Just last night.'

It's too early to soak all of this in, but I'm awake enough to know I don't like it. It's true that my trust in Ruby's good character has been up and down since we met, but I don't like that she's been lingering on our street after I told her to leave. Being the kind-hearted fool that I am, I try putting myself in her position and quickly find I wouldn't be able to tear myself away from Amy as quickly as she was expected to. I mean, that's her daughter, after all.

The taste in my mouth turns to bile. That thought disgusts me so much – Amy is *my* daughter. It doesn't matter where she came from. What's important is that she legally belongs to us, and we've raised her as our own. She's had our love, our food, our company, and – at least until the past few days – our protection.

But what is this that we've exposed her to? A stranger who invades our home with her manipulation and then stirs up trouble between my husband and me? A bizarre lady who sleeps in her car and watches our house as we sleep?

The thought of it makes me cold.

'Thanks, Ed,' I say, closing the door. 'I'll keep an eye out.'

As soon as the door is shut and I'm alone in this empty hall with nothing but an irritating grandfather clock for company, I suddenly feel isolated and vulnerable, as if there's no longer such a thing as privacy. Amy is right upstairs, so at least I know she's safe, but... is she?

I'll go up and check.

Just in case.

Even if only the once, nothing would please me more than to stay home in yesterday's clothes and lounge around while Amy plays with her toys. It works all the way up until lunchtime, when ham sandwiches and some fruit stop her long enough to make her realise she hasn't been out today. Chris and I have always been more 'indoorsy' people, so there's no telling why she likes being outside so much. Unless it's genetic, of course.

After lunch, the questions begin.

'Where are we going today?' Amy asks, scaling the arm of the sofa.

I look up from the magazine long enough to give her the eye – a singular look that tells her to stop climbing the furniture. I wait until she moodily slides off before replying. 'I suppose that depends where you *want* to go.'

'You decide.'

'The park?'

'We go there all the time.'

'For a walk?'

'Boring.'

'How about we go into town?'

'And do what?'

That question stumps me because, aside from places to eat and the occasional drinking venue, I don't really know anywhere to go. Nothing for kids except the aquarium (which we've done too much) and the zoo (which I heard has shut its doors for good anyway). In fact, I'm having trouble thinking of a single thing. Nothing new anyway.

'How about I let you pick out a toy?' I try.

Amy's face lights up, a smile breaking the surface as she stiffens. 'Anything I want?'

'Within reason, yes.'

'I'll get my shoes!'

She darts off at the speed of light while I slap down the magazine that is two weeks old and I haven't had time to read. My head feels foggy as I go upstairs to splash some water on my face, change clothes, and smack a brush through my dry hair. God, I look a state. Like I've been dragged through a thorny bush and only stopped because a brick wall was there to greet me. No amount of make-up will save me – only a stress-free day could ease some of the tension in my face, and that doesn't seem likely while Chris is gone.

Chris.

He's all I've been thinking about, at least when

Ruby isn't on my mind. Throughout the rest of the day, I try pushing them both to the back of my mind while Amy excitedly speeds through multiple toy shops, umm-ing and ahh-ing about which toy she should spend her one wish on. I told her it has to be within reason, but truthfully, I don't care what she picks out. As long as it keeps her occupied and happy while I feel sorry for myself, she can have whatever she likes. I've desperately needed the time to reflect anyway.

After an hour or so of searching, she finally settles on some VTech laptop for kids. The box says it's suitable for her age, so I take it to the till and pay the extortionate price, then let her hug it to her chest while we make our way to the upstairs of the mall and enjoy a coffee and a slice of cake. Juice for Amy, of course.

It's no good though. My wonderful company does nothing to stop me from thinking about Chris. Did he really try paying Ruby for sex, and did he ever try to contact those women who left their numbers? And what about Ruby anyway? Has she really been spying on us?

I never fully trusted her, but I did want to see the best in her. That's a fault of mine that I'd very much like to address – I'm too kind to people, even if they treat me like crap. Although I suspect it's too late now, I'd like a second chance at telling Ruby where to go – that she's not welcome in my home or anywhere near my daughter.

My daughter, I remind myself as I study Amy chomping on a brownie with a line of saliva trailing down her chin. She's so focused on eating it while staring through the glass wall of the coffee shop that she doesn't notice me watching her admirably. Which is a good thing because she doesn't like me staring. Especially when I have this one possessive word on the brain.

Mine.

LIKE ALL GOOD days in recent memory, this one is ruined as well.

Only this time, it's not by Chris or Ed. It's not even by something Ruby has said or done – at least not on this particular day – but her general presence outside my house fills me with enough hot fury to make my blood feel like fire as it rushes through me. I'm not even out of the car before I start swearing under my breath. I barely realise I'm doing it until Amy tells me I've said some 'bad-language words'.

'Sorry, sweetheart. Do me a favour and stay in the car for a minute, okay?'

She doesn't say anything – doesn't need to when her new VTech toy can keep her company with all its lights and colours and interactive whatever-the-hells. I step out of the car and into the freezing wind that shoots up our street like a funnel. Locking the car door instantly, I storm towards Ruby, who still hasn't noticed me. She's too busy staring up at the windows from our doorstep, then leaning forward to knock once again.

'Nobody's home,' I say upon approach.

Ruby turns with a smile, but it fades as soon as she sees the look on my face. If it resembles how I feel, it's probably all twisted up with anger and seething with the shock of seeing Amy's birth mother intruding once again.

'Lizzie. I was just hoping to talk.'

'You've already met your talking quota.'

'Please, I just want to—'

'Save it.' I clench my hands so hard that my nails, although trim, are cutting into my palm. I'm by no means a violent person, but if I ever were to be, it would be for Ruby. 'Ever since the moment you turned up, there's been nothing but trouble in my life.'

'That's not what I wanted.'

'Who cares? It's what ended up happening. And now I hear you're spying on us, too.'

'Spying?' Ruby looks genuinely confused. 'When? Who told you that?'

'Never mind who told me. Have you, or have you not, been watching the house?'

'Of course not. I would never—'

'But you're still parked on the street!' I point at her car, which is easily visible now that the sun has risen. Ruby's eyes follow my finger as if I'm showing her something new, which aggravates me for a reason I don't even know. 'Admit it, you've been spying on us.'

Ruby sighs, and a waft of unclean breath assails me. She must have been in that car all night and hasn't brushed her teeth. A few days ago, I might have invited her in to freshen up, but I've had all I can have of her.

'I wasn't spying,' she says calmly. 'It's just that I had nowhere else to go.'

'Because you're homeless, right?'

'Exactly.'

'So then, the whole world could be your home. Why here? Why this street?'

Ruby shrugs. 'It... feels familiar. Comfortable.'

Frustrated, I look back at my car and see Amy with her face buried in her toy laptop thing. I'm so glad there's a wall and street light between her and Ruby – the last thing I need is for them to start embracing and confusing everything. I don't want anything to stand in the way of the thing I need to do. The thing that will take all of my courage and will.

'You need to leave,' I say, turning back to Ruby. 'And I don't just mean the house. Take your car and get far, far away from here. If you don't, I'll call the police and tell them everything. *Everything*.'

Ruby's mouth is a huge O of surprise. I don't think she ever expected me to defend myself like this, but now that she's faced with it, she doesn't know what to do. I let the silence do the talking, waiting and praying for her to take a step away from my house. When she does, it's slow and unsteady while she seems to size me up. It feels like she's about to lash out at me, but finally, her features soften, and she just nods.

'I'm leaving,' she says, then steps around me and heads for her car.

She doesn't look back as she goes, nor does she peer inside my car to see Amy just a few feet away. It's like she doesn't care, and I can't figure out why that is. It's not until she's gone that I realise it's because she doesn't *need* to care.

It's as if she thinks she'll see Amy again.

Chapter 22
Before…

HAVE you ever had something so close and known you couldn't keep it?

That's what I did when I held Amy for the first time.

She didn't legally have a name yet, but I told the midwife I wanted the kid to be named after her – after the woman who helped me through a twenty-six-hour labour with all the professionalism and kind-heartedness that I would treat my more anxious clients with. She calmed my nerves, talked me through every step of the way, and administered the drugs when I asked for them. What more could she have done?

Nothing. She did it all.

She cried when I told her, then tried to argue

that she wasn't worthy of the honour. I didn't know much about honour, but I knew it would be offensive not to accept it. I argued, not much in the mood for it because I just wanted to sleep while my tea and toast went down (best toast of my whole life, by the way). It turns out she won, because that woman's name was Helga, and my daughter escaped that unfortunate fate.

The problem is the nurses made the mistake of leaving me alone with my new baby. I remember sitting on the edge of the bed, feeling beaten and broken after the birth. There was a little girl right in front of me, stirring quietly in a small bed on wheels. I wanted to pick her up, but I couldn't bring myself to risk waking her.

That's why I said goodbye from where I sat.

Perched on the edge of the bed, already having rushed into the clothes I'd worn coming in – that felt like a lifetime ago – I gazed down at the beautiful newborn, her eyes just like mine and her skin so soft because it was brand new. I wondered what she would grow up to be like and if she'd have any of her father's traits. In years to come, would that help me figure out who that man was? Would it even point me in the right direction?

It didn't matter. I had to just get it over with.

'I'm so sorry, little one,' I began with a croaky voice from both exhaustion and heartbreak. 'You're brand new, but I already know you deserve so much better than me. Your beady little eyes are perfect. Your chubby little fingers are perfect. You *are perfect, and you're going to find a family who will give you everything you need.'*

There was something else – something I whispered in her ear as I kissed her delicately on her little cheek, scared it would break her. I made her the promise, then checked both ends of the hall and walked as fast as I could without looking back. The further I got, the more I cried, until I burst out of the hospital doors and into the warm, summer-night air and flooded my cheeks with tears. I couldn't breathe. I couldn't think. At least not about anything except the promise I made and how there was no way of breaking it.

The promise that I would come back for her someday.

And that nothing would stop me from taking her back.

Chapter 23
Ruby

My car has become a sort of target. Both Ed and Lizzie know exactly what to look for, as if I'd be waving a giant flag to announce my presence on the street. Maybe even a light-up flag, given how dark it is at this time of night.

I've concealed myself in the shadows across the street, right in the dark spot under a broken street light, in the mouth of an alley that seems to lead around the back of three or four different gardens. I must admit, I'm freezing my bloody boobs off in this weather.

But it's all a part of the plan.

It's just gone seven o'clock when a sixteen-year-old toddles along the street towards Lizzie's house. From what little I can see in the dark, she's painfully thin and has the most boring hair I've ever seen in my life. I'm not one hundred per cent certain she's the old man's granddaughter until she knocks on Lizzie's door and waits for it to open. She's so awkward, lightly kicking the doorstep while she waits and not even having thought about wearing a coat.

Like they say: young, dumb, and full of... superfluous thoughts.

Or something like that.

The door opens. Light floods across the doorstep, and the young girl starts to smile. Lizzie welcomes her in, and so begins a long, boring wait out in the not-quite-icy-but-close night air. I can't stop thinking about the babysitter. At that age, they'll believe almost anything they hear, so it shouldn't be too hard to get by her. Failing that, I've had a rough life and know how to handle myself. That girl though? Probably couldn't punch her way out of a wet paper bag.

Bottom line is, this shouldn't be too difficult.

Especially with what's in my pocket.

I was prepared for a long night, but I didn't think it would take this long. I never had experience with a babysitter, but I always thought the parents left as soon as they arrived. Why even bother hanging around after that, except for five minutes where they run through where additional food is, talk about payment and bedtimes, and all the other crap I've only seen in films. What the hell could possibly be taking so long?

Anyway, I've got to be patient. That's what I told myself when I went into all of this. That's what I told *him*, and it can't be one rule for him and one for me. It's not fair, and he'd probably kill me for prioritising myself anyway. So, what little tricks did I learn about helping time slide by? There's a very easy one – and I used this often while lying on my back and getting pounded by unenthusiastic clients from time to time – which is to think of a film and start trying to play it out in my head using nothing but my memory. I pick *The Wizard of Oz* but, thankfully, barely make it to the colour change when Dorothy steps out of the house when Lizzie *also* steps out, saying one last thing to the babysitter before she leaves.

I give it five minutes just to make sure Lizzie leaves. All the while, I stand watching the silhouettes glide behind the lit-up living room window. My daughter is in there, I remind myself. There's barely any distance between us, and thanks to dumb luck, I now know there are barely any obstacles either. Just one young and naïve babysitter.

Who's about to have a bad fucking night.

NEEDLESS TO SAY, I look both ways before crossing the street. Not for cars – there rarely are any down here, if you exclude the people parking outside their homes – but because the last thing I need is Ed 'Fuckface' Warner coming out and causing trouble. I just need a clean break. A few minutes to get in, take what I need, then leave.

I walk towards the house with all the confidence in the world. Nothing could possibly go wrong tonight. However I walk away with Amy, all I have to do is get her to my car and get a good head start on my journey. After that, I don't care who comes for me.

It won't be my problem any more.

As soon as I mentally prepare myself, I knock on the door. Even this can't be too aggressive because I don't want the young girl to panic or consider calling someone for help. Everything must be delicate, deliberate, calm.

Unlike the evening ahead of me.

Weirdly, I don't even remember the girl's name

until she opens the door. Almost as if she's wearing a name badge, it comes to me immediately. She even *looks* like a Jess, for crying out loud. If that's possible? It must be, otherwise it wouldn't have sprung out at me like that.

'You all right?' she asks. Such a soft tone. So young. So fragile.

'Maybe. Is Lizzie in?'

'Oh, she's gone out. Sorry.'

'Who are you?' I ask, and there's an awkward pause. I let it linger long enough, giving her time to figure out if she's obligated to answer or not, then butt in at the right moment. 'I'm only asking because I care about Lizzie and Amy's well-being. I'm just making sure you're not an intruder or something.'

The girl's face drops, just as intended. There's no way in hell this trick would work on an adult, but the shock expressed by her open mouth tells me I've got nothing to worry about. I'm counting down the seconds until *she* tries to earn *my* trust.

'Oh, I'm Amy's babysitter. You can ask Lizzie if you don't believe me.'

Bingo.

'Nah, that won't be necessary,' I tell her with a smile, offering comfort and reassurance in my friendliest tone. 'It's not like she would just let any old stranger into her home. So if you're sure I can trust you, there's no need for me to run a check.'

'You can trust me.'

'Good. I left my phone charger here earlier. Can I come and get it?'

A slight hesitation.

'What does it look like?'

'A phone charger,' I say with a giggle. 'Black but with a little red coil.'

'I haven't seen it.'

'Can I just come in and check? I won't disturb Amy.'

'Oh. Erm...'

I tell her it's fine and then move to step inside the house. The idea is to seize control – to let her know that she may be in charge of Amy, but she's not in charge of me, and she sure as hell doesn't get to tell me I'm not allowed in the house. It's as easy as moving my foot and flaring my arms to take up more space and be assertive, but it doesn't work.

She pushes the door slightly shut, blocking my path.

The shock of it grounds me.

We exchange a hard stare.

'Is there a problem here?' I ask, furrowing my brow.

'Sorry, I can't just let someone in.'

'It's just for a charger, Jess.'

Another pause, this one putting me under the spotlight.

'How do you know my name?'

Thinking on my feet, I take a small step back to let her know I'm not a threat as I try to undo the situation. It's already on its way to failure, but there's no harm in giving it one last try before resorting to violence. That's only fair, isn't it?

'Lizzie has mentioned you,' I explain, 'but I didn't realise you were here.'

'Oh yeah? What did she say about me?'

'Just that she knows your grandfather and you needed some extra cash.'

Jess's eyes roll all the way down to my feet before drifting back up. She's trying to see if I'm trouble, and I loosen my stiff posture, hoping it will encourage her to relax. She hasn't said anything yet, so I beat her to it and try to gain control again.

'Look, all I wanted was my charger. If you're going to make this difficult, then I'll just give Lizzie a call and interrupt her night. But I want you to know in advance that I won't be holding back in letting her know exactly *why* I had to call.'

I'm bluffing, of course, and try to sell it by pulling out my phone and making out as if I intend to call. Jess should have stopped me seconds ago, panicking that I've cost her a babysitting gig, but the time rolls by without her saying a word.

She's calling my bluff.

And that's bad news for her.

I'm backed into a corner now. My only two options are to walk away or revert to plan B. There's no way in hell I'm leaving here without Amy, so I reach into my pocket and take out my little friend. Jess's eyes widen when she sees it – the glint of light as it strikes the blade. It's three inches long, but the ridges and curves make it look like a hunter's tool.

Technically, it is.

Before she can shut the door on me, I raise the penknife above my head, ready to attack in a swooping motion – like an eagle seizing its prey. Then I lunge forward, shoving open the door with my free hand as I invade Lizzie's home for the final time.

This time leaving a bloody trail behind me.

. . .

THIS IS IT. I'm finally where I need to be.

Amy's bedroom door is ajar. The landing light is off, but there's enough coming from downstairs to illuminate a small portion of my daughter. She's in her bed, sleeping soundly in a tangle of duvet and pillows. Her pyjamas are keeping her warm enough, so I don't need to worry. I just want to take in this moment of peace.

It won't last too long.

Jess is downstairs, right where she belongs. I don't imagine she'll be a problem. No matter how gobby she feels she has a right to be, my little three-inch friend made her back away with her hands up. I've never seen anyone go from confident to a puddle of tears in such a short space of time. She made it easy to pity her, and yet my knife still got to taste her blood.

Like I said, she won't be a problem.

Time is limited, but I really want to enjoy this moment. I know I have a few minutes before having to leave. Is that enough for me to just take in the peace – the steady rise and fall of little Amy's chest as she takes breaths in her deep sleep? It's such a surreal feeling to watch this girl and know she's mine. She doesn't remotely resemble the baby I left at Cossham Hospital five years ago. The chubby cheeks are gone, the vulnerability having left her eyes. She's bigger, quieter, and has a personality I've come to love.

It's almost a shame I'm about to make her cry.

When it feels like I've started to push my luck, there's nothing left to do but wake her. I step inside the room, the floorboard creaking under my weight. Amy stirs, mumbles something, and then rolls over. I get closer, tiptoeing needlessly towards her so I can smell the sugary-sweet fruity shampoo she must have used tonight. I love that smell. I used to use the same shampoo when I was a kid. At least when we could afford it.

That's not a problem Amy will ever know.

She'll be taken care of like no other kid.

'Amy, sweetie,' I say, kneeling beside her and gently laying a hand on her chest. She stirs again, her eyes softly flickering open while they find me in the dark room. I almost expect her to panic, but she doesn't. She only smiles when I tell her what's happening. 'This is just a dream, okay? It's time we go somewhere better.'

'Somewhere better?' she asks groggily.

'Yes. Anywhere but here.'

There's no refusal or even so much as another question. She just dozes off again and lets me scoop my hands under her light little body. Then, just like I've been meaning to do for many, many years, I lift her up and take her from her bed, her home, her life.

And everyone in it.

Chapter 24
Lizzie

I'M a big ball of nerves.

It's not because I'm leaving Amy with a babysitter for the first time in forever, but because of the circumstances surrounding it. I trust Jess and always have – she's done a great job taking care of my daughter before now, and there's no reason that should change.

Except tonight, I'm extra paranoid.

The Methodist church rents itself out for art classes every night of the week. Mondays are for painting, for example. Saturday is sculpting day, which is probably the most popular, but my attention was always grabbed by the idea of clay modelling. Not to be confused with pottery, mind you – pottery involves pots and vases. Modelling involves everything else.

The hall is large and empty, with stacked plastic chairs lining three of the walls. There's a sterile scent in the air, like bleach but not as strong. I'm standing at my own table, watching the people file in one by one, most of them running late because they're unable to keep to a simple schedule. I won't lie, it winds me up a little. Amy is at home, and although I have no reason to feel guilty for leaving her, I still do.

My hands won't stop twitching. I pick up my phone to check for messages from Jess. There aren't any. That's not unusual, but I'm more on edge than normal. It's because of Ruby, I'm telling you. I'm starting to regret having let her into our lives.

The hall finally gets filled, and our leader – who insists on being called a teacher, but nobody has yet complied – stands at the front of the class. She's a kindly old lady with a warm face, but I wouldn't like to upset her. There's just something about her that suggests she'd snap at you if you spoke to her in the wrong tone of voice.

Today, she lifts a blanket off a small clay sculpture. This happens every week, becoming some kind of ritualistic reveal of what we're all supposed to be imitating. There's usually a person or vehicle or something easy like that, but today, I'm staring hopelessly at a small grey wolf on its hindquarters. There's no way I could match her level of detail.

I might as well leave right now.

But I don't. I've missed this class far too often to just walk out of here tonight. That's the only reason I'm staying because God knows I'm dying to just grab my handbag and head for the door. Still, my compulsion to check on Amy gets the better of me, so I pick up my phone one last time and send a text before muddying my hands with wet clay:

Hi Jess. Just checking in. Everything okay?

That's all it takes. It might be five minutes before I get a reply, or it could be a couple of hours. The best I can do is put it out of my mind by focusing on whatever limp version of a clay wolf I'm supposed to sculpt from a large wet blob. It should be nice – a good distraction from all the crap that's happened lately and all the irrational worries haunting my fragile brain. That's the way it *should* be anyway. But there's something else occupying my mind.

I just can't shake the feeling that something is seriously wrong.

THE WOLF IS DONE to the best of my abilities. It doesn't look anything like the one our leader made – its four legs are thick and chunky because I couldn't get it to stand otherwise. The tail also created an imbalance, and by the time I made that, I'd pretty much given up on the fur detailing. What I'm left with is a lazy cross-breed between a clay wolf and a grey slug.

It's my brain's fault. I haven't stopped thinking about Amy and the situation with Ruby. At least Jess replied to me and said everything was just fine, although that was a while ago. It's tempting to check again, but I didn't want to disrupt the class. Not with the way our leader gawks at me whenever I look at my phone.

At least it's at its end. Everyone has labelled their models and submitted them to the box. They'll go to the kiln while we're away, ready for us to paint during our next session. I'm not entirely sure I'll even attend. It's been ages since I came to the last one, and the only reason I came tonight was to see if I could get comfortable being away from Amy.

It turns out I can't.

The other sculptors stick around for coffee and biscuits, but I just want to go home. I tell them I'm not feeling great, rummaging through my handbag for the car keys as I head outside. I'm only a few steps out of the door before I bump into someone I really didn't want to see. At least not for a few more days.

'Hi, Lizzie.'

I step back and look down at my feet, just so I don't have to look at his eyes. However, the silence between us only grows more uncomfortable when the bitter wind picks up. I finally meet Chris's gaze, struck by how handsome he is but at the same time full of resentment for all that's happened. I'm starting to wonder if we can go back to what we were.

Or even something close.

'What are you doing here?' I ask, trying not to sound as annoyed as I feel.

'All I want is to talk, and I figured you'd be here.'

'So you thought you'd come and disrupt my evening?'

'No, I just want to talk.'

'Chris, I—'

'Sorry. I'm... sorry.' Chris holds up a hand to pause me, tilting his head down to reset before trying a new approach. 'I didn't mean to ruin your evening, and I definitely don't mean to upset you, but can we just talk for a minute or two?'

I shake my head slowly, not because he doesn't deserve a conversation but because my mind is more fixed on getting home to Amy than anything. But while he reads my reaction, Chris stays quiet and pays me the respect I feel I deserve... by not saying another word.

'There's been so much disruption lately,' I tell him. 'Not much of it was caused by you, but you have to see this from my perspective. All these issues mounted up in such a short space of time. I barely had time to deal with any one of them.'

'I'd sooner blame Ruby for those.'

'And I've told her as much. She's gone for good.'

'How can you be so sure?'

Something about the way he said it makes me pause. 'Do you know something I don't?'

'Not at all, only that she seems far too persistent to just get up and leave. Lizzie, look, I really just want a chance to explain those phone numbers you found. If you'll just give me a couple of minutes, then I'll walk away until you're ready to make the big decision.'

It's weird to hear the simplicity of it – that our marriage could end any minute now, and it's all hinging on whatever I say next. With such a life-changing choice ahead of us, it's hard to deny that my husband – the man I swore I'd do anything for – doesn't at least deserve a chance. Even if just a very small one.

'I'll drive you back to wherever you're staying,' I tell him. 'As soon as we get there, we stop talking about it, and you leave me alone to process everything. Deal?'

Chris's face lights up, his hope restored. 'Deal. But if I don't have anywhere yet?'

'You're homeless?'

'I'm using a truck.'

'Then I'll just drive home. That's when our conversation ends. You can walk from there.'

'Deal,' he says again before stepping aside and gesturing towards the car park.

By now, the other sculptors are exiting the building. We live in such a small and friendly area that most of them know Chris and offer him a pleasant smile as they pass. He returns in kind, then follows me to my car while I wonder if I've made the right choice.

It's not a long drive home, but it feels like it.

Chris has already told me the story of the women who gave him their numbers. Although he couldn't speak for them, it was apparent they were physically attracted to him just by the mere fact they offered their details to him on a platter. He never acted on them, he tells me, and he never intended to.

Of course, I questioned why he bothered to keep them.

'I just never got around to throwing them out,' he says.

'That's convenient.'

'Think about it. If I had something to hide or even wanted to contact them, wouldn't I just add those numbers to my phone? Wouldn't I have done something then and there while I was out on the road and could get away with it?'

The phrasing makes me jerk the steering wheel a little too hard. I lean forward to peer through the windscreen at the dark road, somehow concentrating on both my driving and the conversation. He's right – he could have easily kept them from me. Although I suppose he did, at least until Ruby stumbled upon them.

'Lizzie, please understand I would never cheat on you.'

'I believe you,' I say, and it's the truth.

'So can you forgive me for not telling you about those women?'

'Maybe.'

'Thank you. For what it's worth, I love you and all your...'

It's not that he stops talking – it's that it *seems* as though he does. Ahead of us, my front door draws attention away from his words until he's barely a muffle in the background. When I hear him make a confused grunt, I conclude he must be seeing the same thing I am. The same heart-stopping, life-altering shape of our doorway, the hallway light spilling through the open door. The door that swings in the wind as if being toyed with by a ghost.

'Isn't Jess...?' he starts.

'She's supposed to be.'

I don't waste time parking the car. Hell, I don't even get the keys out of the ignition. My body feels weightless as I burst into the open air and pound towards my house. The entire time, my legs feel like they're about to give in. Heat burns up my cheeks, and my chest feels tight. Terror pinches at my spine, and it would be enough to stop me if Chris weren't here to protect me. That, and the fact I have somebody in the house to protect.

'Amy,' I expel in a cloud of warm mist.

The house feels empty as I enter. It shouldn't be this quiet. There should be the chuckle of a young girl who refuses to go to bed. There should be the frustrated commands of a babysitter who's barely in control. The hallway should be filled with my presence, but instead, it feels like I'm a weightless ghost observing a crime scene. One I can't interfere with.

When I see the blood, the hairs stand up on the back of my neck. Chris rushes in beside me, sees what I see, then follows the trail through the house. It happens in a blur, my legs turning to jelly while I experience unbeatable guilt for wishing it's Jess's blood.

Just so it won't be Amy's.

I'm at the bottom stairs before I know it, taking them two steps at a time while my heart beats triple its normal rate. Amy's bedroom door is ajar – *no blood, thank God* – and I burst inside. The light blinds me, my hand rising to cover my eyes just enough. I think my brain is subtly telling me not to look – that I won't like what I see when I tear my hand away and look at where Amy is sleeping.

No, to where she *slept*.

My entire life falls to pieces in an instant. I finally collapse, my back hitting the door frame as I move my mouth to call Chris. The words don't come, but a dumb rasp wheezes through my teeth as I stare helplessly at my daughter's empty bed.

'She's gone,' I try and struggle to say in its entirety. 'Amy... she's gone.'

Chapter 25
Ruby

AMY JOLTS AWAKE as we drive over a pothole. The Mondeo dips and jumps, the tyres taking a pounding as the car rolls over the concrete and slides through the open gates of a large, abandoned warehouse. She sits up and takes notice, scanning her surroundings as if she's just been plucked from one space and time to another.

I suppose that's half true.

'Where are we?' she asks, rubbing her eyes and yawning.

There's no way to answer that without giving her the grim truth, so I keep quiet and stay focused on the gravel path that leads towards the buildings. They lurk there like tall figures of judgement, as if they're about to either let me pass or condemn me for my sins.

My biggest sin being extremely recent.

The police must be after me by now. I can only imagine Lizzie returning from her class to find the bloody mess I left behind. Her face must be a picture of raw shock when she goes to the bedroom and finds her (my) daughter missing from her bed. I would laugh about my victory if my conscience weren't so damn fragile. At the end of the day, Lizzie was good to me. Not so good that it stopped me from doing what I wanted, but it was definitely enough to make me feel bad about it.

Especially with what comes next.

'I would like to formally request my return to home,' Amy says bravely, trying to mask the quiver of fear in her voice. It lasts all of five seconds before she crumbles. 'Please, Ruby. Take me home. I'm cold and scared and don't know where we are.'

Great, I think. *Make me feel even worse.*

Once again, I ignore my daughter and continue driving towards the buildings. Through the rising fog, there's very little to see except the headlights that cut through it, occasionally highlighting a shape I instantly mistake for a human being.

Eventually, I find the meeting spot around the back. Amy is in a full flood of tears now. I tell her it's going to be okay – that's right, I lie to her – and then slowly bring the car to a crawl around the back of the buildings. Nobody will see us here, which makes even me a little nervous. It's been a long time since I've seen *him*, and so much has happened.

So much is *about* to happen.

I find a quiet spot and kill the engine. Amy desperately grabs my arm and looks at me with pleading puppy-dog eyes. It's torture, not just for her but for me. This wasn't really what I wanted to happen, but what choice did I have?

I deserve to get what I want.

'Ruby?' Amy asks, her voice now a whimper. 'What's happening?'

'Just stay calm, and everything will be fine,' I tell her.

'Can we go home?'

'No.'

'I want my mum.'

A part of me wants to tell her the truth – that she's sitting with her mum right now – but what's the point? With how things are about to go, it's best she knows as little as possible. It would only upset her more anyway. Not to mention how miserable it would make me feel.

We sit and wait for too long. The silence is unbearable, but the darkness is my ally. I feel concealed, like the rest of the world can't touch me for the time being. It provides a sense of safety I've never truly experienced.

But how long will it last?

WE WAIT IN THE SHADOWS, the mist sneaking around us to engulf the car like a majestic cloud. I haven't said anything in a long time, and neither has Amy. She's just trying the door occasionally, stopped by the child lock and too embarrassed to complain about it. She brings her knees to her chest and tries to hide her shivers. They're not shivers of cold – I turned the heating back on a few minutes ago, and the inside of the car is toasty.

These are shivers of fear.

For the record, it doesn't satisfy me to treat a kid like this. It's not something I'm proud of, and I wouldn't be doing it at all if I didn't have to. But Amy is mine, and I can do what I like with her. It's a free world after all, isn't it? Or is that just what I always told myself growing up? It definitely helped when entering the prostitution ring. My conscience had less to wrestle with once I started ignoring the law entirely.

Old habits die hard, eh?

It takes about thirty more minutes before the shadows shift in the night. Weirdly, I don't see the headlights until they slip through the fog and turn onto the property. There are six of them, like the eyes of three horsemen coming to claim their prize. It makes me wonder.

Where is the fourth?

One of the cars departs from the others and hides behind the abandoned warehouse. The other two do a drive-by for security and then park opposite me. My breath is caught in my throat right now because there's no telling how this will go. Horribly wrong is what I imagine, but there's always that small chance everything will work out just fine.

Regardless, I'm not in control of the situation.

'Ruby?' Amy asks in a frail whisper. 'Who are they?'

'Friends,' I lie, followed by another. 'Everything will be all right.'

She doesn't argue, and I don't encourage her to. My eyes are trained on the two cars parked ahead of us, and I guess *he* is sitting in the third one. It's typical of him to leave the work to his lackeys, but whatever. As long as it's handled, who am I to argue?

The cars' engines shut off. One of them gives a dying flash of its headlights first, signalling me to make the approach. I've never been this scared in my life, and that's saying something. My hands are shaking so violently it almost looks exaggerated.

I turn to Amy. 'I need to get out and talk to these people. You just need to stay here and be a good girl, okay? No matter what happens, don't leave the car.'

'Ruby,' she whines.

'No, just listen. You might get scared, but trust me when I say you're safe. See these people?' I point at the cars and try to ignore the sparkle of tears in my daughter's eyes. 'They're not going to hurt you, but the less trouble you cause, the better. So just do everything they say, and I promise everything will go smoothly. Do you understand?'

Amy begins to cry, of course. Who wouldn't? She's five years old, for crying out loud.

Before her tears turn to pitiful sobbing, I exit the car and lock the doors. Then, I approach the other vehicles slowly, apprehensively. There's movement ahead – a door opening in the swirling, smoke-like fog that breaks at its mercy. A figure steps out, then another from the passenger side. We meet somewhere in the middle, but they're only voices in the darkness.

'Did you bring her?' one of them asks.

'In the car.'

'The key?'

I hesitate for only a second – that would be my conscience doing a number on me after ripping her from Lizzie – then hand over the car key. As soon as it's done, I'm expecting the payment. A sum big enough that I forget about the clothes and other possessions I've left for them to dispose of. I can buy new ones, as long as these guys pay up.

As long as *he* pays up.

'The payment?' I ask in a nervous croak, shifting my stare from one to the other and then back again. It truly looks as though they're not going to pay – like they'll finish me off right here and now if only to leave no loose ends. But when they step aside and point towards the corner of the old warehouse, it looks like I might live to see tomorrow. 'That way?'

'Right around the corner. Don't keep him waiting.'

I nod and am surprised they let me walk. It's a

harsh feeling though – the further I get from Amy, the worse I feel. Whether I like it or not, I immediately fell in love with Amy. Maybe that's the genetic connection talking, but it feels real enough for me, and that only makes it harder to leave her behind.

Still, it doesn't stop me from searching for *him*.

THE CAR IS where I was told it would be. It lurks there in the darkness like a predator stalking its prey. A singular man steps out and waves me over impatiently. I stand on the corner and look at the other men, my Mondeo, and Amy. For the first time tonight, I wonder if I'm safe.

But there's no turning back now.

As I make my way towards the car, the man opens the rear door and holds it for me. I don't thank him as I enter – just turn my nose up at his overpowering cologne that smells like vinegar and climb into the back seat beside *him*. Beside the man who always smells like honey and elderflower. The man who created this whole dramatic situation to begin with.

'It's about time,' he says moodily.

All I know about this man is that his name is

John. He was a client of mine when I was younger. *Much* younger. Back when I was someone else's little girl and needed some extra money just to keep a roof over my head. John made his presence known to me, introduced me to a man who I guess you could call my pimp, and then left. Over the years, he would come by every few weeks just to collect some money. Would that make him my pimp's pimp?

Pimpception, I think humourlessly.

John only had his way with me three times, and each of those times was identical. He put me on my back and did his business without so much as a change of expression. He hated me, I could tell even back then, and he still has that same look right now: frosty and fed up, his lips almost peeling back with anger as he hands over a padded envelope.

'Count it,' he says, then drops it into my lap.

The weight of it hits my leg. It's heavy, so it must be at least close to what we bargained for. I don't think John would rip me off, so I will definitely count it... but right now, I'm just staring at his oddly youthful face. He always looked to me like one of those men you'd see advertising winter clothing, donning an expensive business suit but covering it up with a long coat that suggested he meant... well, business. The only thing that's changed over the years is that his ruggedness has increased with grey stubble and a faintly receding hairline. He's actually extremely handsome. It's a shame he's a piece of work.

'I told you to count it,' he snaps with an impatient sigh.

'Yeah, yeah.'

The envelope's flap opens. A wad of cash falls out. There has to be over fifteen thousand pounds in here, and I'm not going to flicker through every last note to make sure he's kept to his end of the bargain. I pinch out thirty notes, eye up the thickness of that pile, then use it as a guide to measure the rest. I managed to count approximately fourteen thousand, so there's no reason to believe I've been short-changed. You could say it's right on the money.

The problem is I haven't been truthful.

When we first struck this deal, I told him I wanted to take the cash and then start a new life somewhere up north. I said I didn't give a crap about Amy – she was just a child I didn't really know or feel for. But that wasn't true. It especially isn't now that I've met and had interactions with her. Honestly, this money just feels tainted. *Dirty*.

For John, it was supposed to be an easy transaction. He's done this so many times that it's probably just a regular Tuesday for him. Amy would be groomed just like all those other girls were. Just like *I* was. Then she'd be thrown into his multi-branch prostitution ring, perhaps even auctioned off to the highest bidder – some sick, rich paedophile who felt entitled to have his way with anyone, despite their age. John always took care of his girls, fed them, made sure they had money and work, but the problem is he never saw them as girls. Not even as people.

They were his products.

But it was never supposed to get this far.

My stomach knots at the thought of Amy's future. When I first overheard John mention that he needed some 'younger models', my ears pricked up, and I instantly thought about my daughter. It seemed ideal at the time, because I had a girl out there somewhere, and I knew he would pay me. I approached him then and there, right on the top floor of that grotty little whorehouse, and told him I could bring him a five-year-old. He agreed instantly, emotionlessly, as if it was all purely business. Perhaps that was what made it so easy for me to disregard Amy's future. It all felt so calm and smooth.

But I was never going to give her up. I thought I could take the money and run, but the current situation suggests I'd never get away with something like that. Not with all these men around. I realise now that I've sealed her fate, then frantically try to undo it.

'I want something else,' I tell him, putting on a brave face.

John rolls his eyes, checks his watch, then waves a hand for me to go on. I'm almost certain I'm going to regret saying this, but what other choice do I have? I put Amy right in harm's way, and if I let her go now, I'd never be able to sleep at night.

That's why I take a deep breath of courage.

Then make my request.

Chapter 26
Lizzie

Amy has been gone for twenty to thirty minutes. That's what Jess said when Chris found her, curled up and crying on the kitchen floor. She wasn't killed – wasn't even harmed that much, really – but had slashes across her wrists where she raised her arms to protect herself. I feel horrendously guilty, of course, but the police keep reminding me it wasn't me who did it.

It was Ruby.

Our home has been invaded more than once tonight. The police and their team came in to briefly examine the place. Chris and I spend the whole time outside in the cold, embracing each other while we wait and pray they'll find our little girl. Meanwhile, Jess is getting patched up on the back step of a nearby ambulance, and half the street is out to assess the drama. If I wasn't so frozen with fear for Amy's well-being, I'd be hurling rocks at them all by now.

When it's safe to go back inside, the police sit us down to ask some more questions. They're mostly a retread of what they've already asked, and I don't think I can take much more of this. Chris takes the reins, holding me close while I lean into him and suddenly forget that we ever had an argument. Who cares about sluts on the road when our girl is gone?

Gone.

The thought sparks new fear inside me, slamming me with the reality of what's happened. But it's not just the absence that hurts. It's the guilt of knowing I let Ruby come this far. I let her into our home and treated her like a member of the family. If I knew she was going to kidnap my daughter, I would have bitch-slapped her and sent her on her way immediately.

But it's not me who has to pay the consequences of my actions.

It's Amy.

The police finally conclude their business and promise they'll do everything they can to find her.

They don't sound hopeful, and why should they? Nobody has even the faintest clue where Ruby has gone, and she doesn't have a home address. Even the adoption agency has Amy's mother listed as unknown.

As soon as the door is shut, I burst into a fit of tears. Chris comes to hold me once more, and although it feels safe, it doesn't feel like home any more. You can factor in the big house, even count all our worldly possessions, but without the cheerful melody of Amy's giggle and the quirky questions she used to spring upon us, this is nothing but a hollow building.

It will never be home until she returns.

If she returns.

The knot in my stomach tightens. Chris reinforces his embrace. For just a few moments, there's nothing in the world outside of this. His hug is strong and comforting, but it will never be enough. I reach around and squeeze his back, but it will never be enough.

Nothing will ever be enough.

A heavy fist raps on the door. I jolt a little but don't move. Chris and I wait in the silence, equally certain it's just one of the nosy neighbours coming to catch up on the latest gossip. It's sick, really. Can't they just leave us to our misery?

The knock comes again. It's harder this time. More persistent. Chris sighs heavily and peels away from me, leaving me cold and exposed. I wrap my arms around my chest and let my head sag while he goes to the door, peers through the peephole, then opens it with a sigh.

'Not today, Ed,' he says, and my insides crumble.

The last thing I need is Ed Warner snooping around.

But Ed doesn't say anything. He simply pushes past Chris and steps into the hall, his grey tangle of hair a wired mess. His eyes scan his surroundings until they find me, and then he comes a little closer. My heart is beating against my ribs as he makes his approach. I start to turn away because I don't want to deal with him right now.

As if I have a choice.

'I'm awfully sorry to hear about your girl,' Ed says, looking me dead in the eye and holding a sincerity I've never seen before. But there's something about this that makes me uncomfortable. Something knowing. 'Do the police know what happened?'

I look to Chris, mostly because I don't feel like talking, but I wouldn't know what to say if I did. Chris shrugs, takes a single step forward as if about to act on it, then stops himself. I then nod, and he takes another step before putting a hand on Ed's shoulder.

'Now's not the time,' he says calmly, soothingly.

'I just wanted to express—'

'Yes, but now is not the time.'

Ed looks at me without an inch of movement. For some reason I can't quite understand, he has me captivated – locked into his steely gaze and having me ask a thousand questions without uttering a single word. What follows is a world of silence where everything stands still. Everything is fine in this world – it's comfortable, possibly because it offers hope. I think Ed knows something, but I'm too scared to ask. I don't want to be shot down or to have my most desperate wish obliterated by simply being told no.

'Ed,' Chris says with a hint of impatience. 'Now's not a good time.'

'It's the perfect time. I would like to talk about Ruby.'

'You've done enough talking about that bloody woman.'

'Yes, but that's because she's bad news.'

'Hate to tell you this, but you're not exactly *good* news.'

I can tell Chris is at the end of his tether because he hisses these last few words. The hand on Ed's shoulders tightens its vice-like grip, pulling him away with more force than an elderly man can endure. He stumbles slightly as Chris yanks him back towards the door. There's not a single part of me that wants to help him – all I can think about is Amy.

'You don't understand,' he protests as he's dragged away, but Chris doesn't hold back in his intention to get our nosy old neighbour out of our hair. 'Please, Chris, just let me ask a couple of things, and I'll be on my way.'

These last words drive me insane. I scoff and turn my back on him, my hope of him having some valuable information completely ripped away from me. I'm facing the wall where pictures of a younger Amy hang, her gap-toothed smile endearing and heart-shattering at the same time. I don't know what to do or where to look.

Until Ed spits out his most desperate plea, leading me to a sharp intake of breath.

'I think I know where Amy is!'

'What the hell did you just say?'

Chris's voice booms through the house so loud it even makes *me* jump. I spin around on my heel. The hand that's been pressing a tissue to my nose lowers, as does my jaw. Chris has let go of Ed, and they're both standing by the door. Although Ed has his back against the wall beside it, the old man held captive by my angry husband.

'It's true,' Ed says solemnly. 'Perhaps we can sit so I can explain?'

I don't feel like sitting – I feel like pacing and maybe even punching something. Or some*one*. But as much as it feels like fiction (or just the ramblings of a delusional old fool), it's impossible to resist further enquiry. Chris is waiting on me, staring directly into my eyes as if to read my reaction. He's waiting for me to say something: yes or no.

Like I said, I can't resist.

'Kitchen,' I say in one of my less patient tones.

I walk in and drag a chair out from under the dining table. The wooden legs screech against the tiles in protest, leaving a long, white line across the floor. Chris enters with Ed a moment later, forcing him into the chair like a tough city cop from one of those TV dramas.

'Sit,' he spits like Ed isn't already doing exactly that.

Ed wobbles in the wooden chair as he tries to stay upright. It's too forceful for a man of his age, but I don't give a crap. You can't come into my home and drop a bombshell like that about my missing daughter without explaining yourself. Especially as we've had the police here, digging for information anywhere they can get it.

'Well?' I say, allowing him to delve deeper into his previous statement.

'It's not what you think it is,' he says, briefly craning his neck to look at Chris, who's standing guard behind him with his arms crossed. Then he turns to me, once more looking into my soul with those piercing eyes. 'Before I tell you anything, you have to promise not to call the police. Only then can I fully explain.'

Chris snaps out a hand and strikes Ed on the back, gritting his teeth.

'Out with it,' he says.

Ed nods quickly, his hands shaking. 'The truth is, I've known your mysterious house guest for a lot longer than you might think. Which also means I know an awful lot about her.'

'What are you talking about?' I ask.

'Well, she used to... I mean, I... Life gets very lonely sometimes.'

'You paid for her services?' Chris asks.

'Many years ago. Back when she was younger.'

'How young?'

'*Too* young. She probably doesn't remember me.'

I roll my eyes, not entirely surprised to hear that Ed is something of a pervert. Not that hiring a prostitute necessarily puts him in that box, but to hire a young lady when she's just trying to make her way in the world? It suddenly explains a lot.

Chris takes the lead. 'Right, so you know what exactly?'

'I know she used to work out of a building in town, right near the train station. That was where I used to go back then, looking for company. That building was always full of women just like her, and they would talk more loudly than they should.'

'Get to the point,' I snap.

'Okay, okay. Well, there was a man who used to come by every now and then. I don't know what his name is or even what he looked like – I only heard his voice. They would talk about exchanges, acquiring "new talent" from women who might not want to be hired. *Young* women, if you get what I'm trying to say.'

I do, and it makes my stomach churn. Is that what's happening to Amy? Is she being passed on to follow in her mother's footsteps? My little girl, barely old enough to understand basic algebra, being put out to market by her birth mother and some old creep?

'Please don't tell me you're saying what I think you're saying.' My breath leaves me with those words, my chest feeling so tight I might suffocate.

'I'm afraid so, dear.' Ed shakes his head and lowers it in shame. 'But I also know where they used to meet for these exchanges. At least, that was the case many years ago. As long as they haven't switched things up, there's an old warehouse in Kingswood where they like to do things in private. I'll write down the address if you'll give me a pen and —'

'Why didn't you tell this to the police?' I ask. 'They were right here.'

'Because... well, it's complicated.'

'You don't want to get in trouble,' Chris says. 'There's more to it than you're saying.'

'Yes. Something like that.'

I look to my husband, usually the decision maker of the house. But this time, he's not rushing to say anything – he only glances at his watch and then stares my way, waiting on my response. It's obvious what he's suggesting – that if we're going to trust this dirty old bastard, then we'd better get moving soon.

'Please don't get me into trouble,' Ed says. 'I just don't want your girl to be gone forever.'

Gone forever, I think as another foul taste reaches my tongue. It feels like I just licked a battery, and my nerves feel like they've been electrified. Chris knows what I'm thinking – he always has been able to read me like a book with big, colourful pictures and few words.

It's now or never if we want to get our daughter back.

And the clock is ticking.

Chapter 27
Ruby

JOHN'S EYES widen as I make my request. Even in the dim shadow of the car that's only faintly illuminated by the dome light, he looks like a sly silver fox who can't decide if he's furious or highly impressed by the balls it took to even ask that question.

'I want to know where Amy is at all times,' I said to him. 'Can I see her one last time?' It's the only way I can think of to actually get close to her. What then? Run?

Moments have passed since I asked, but it feels like forever ago. Those ice-cold eyes boring into me suggest he's about to blow a fuse – that I'm about to be evicted from the car without Amy, without money, and quite possibly without my life. The thing is, if I could rewind time, I would ask the same question all over again.

It's because it's Amy. You could say it all felt real the moment the money went into my hands. I feel the weight of it now, and it's lighter than the girl I'm close to exchanging for it. I obviously still want and need it, but if there's a way to do this without giving her up, then the least I could do is try.

'Let me get this straight,' John says, shifting uncomfortably in his rich-leather car seat. 'I asked you to deliver me a new asset in exchange for a small sum. You took your damn precious time delivering the goods, left me waiting without much explanation, and then finally brought her to me. Now that you have the money, you think you're in a position to keep the goods in your life while also running off with the cash?'

I don't answer because it's rhetorical. This isn't going the way I hoped it would, and there's probably no way to change it. But I can't back-pedal either – the thought of a life without Amy sounds like absolute torture. Is this how Lizzie must feel when she inevitably goes years without knowing where her little girl is?

My little girl, I remind myself all over again.

'I just want a few last words with her,' I tell him.

'No.' It's as simple as that. Cold, blunt, no. 'The moment that money went into your hands, the girl became my property. Your involvement in her life ends there.'

The strangest feeling comes over me now. A deep shuddering in my soul. A weakness in my knees that makes me appreciate the fact I'm sitting down. Then, in the corner of my eye, the slight moisture of a tear I never saw coming.

'Don't tell me you've developed a sense of emotion.' John lazily fakes a laugh. 'So we're clear, you're going to stop working for me and get the hell out of Bristol. You've got your money, so put it to good use.'

'What about Amy?' I ask.

'Is that her name?'

'Please tell me what exactly will happen to her.'

'You already know. You went through it yourself.'

'I want to see her,' I say again, this time through the choke of tears.

'You don't hear the word "no" often, do you?'

'Please let me just say goodbye.'

'I suppose you think this is your right?'

There's nothing left for me to say. I've made my request, and it's all in his hands. John eyes me, still clinging onto that confused mix of surprise and pride. I've asked for something nobody else would ever dare ask, and now the ball is in his court.

Suddenly, he takes a breath and delivers his answer.

By the time we get back to the car, the other men have surrounded it. They seem to be guarding it with their lives, like stone gargoyles sworn to defend the vehicle and its contents with their lives. I wonder for a moment if they'll ever let me get past them, but then I remember John is their boss. Whatever he says goes.

'Move,' he tells them, then turns to me. 'You get two minutes.'

'What happens after two minutes?' I ask.

'She becomes mine, and you fuck off.'

I swallow hard, but there's no moisture in my throat. It's all dry and raspy, like a cactus is stuck in there. The men part like the Red Sea, and I open the driver-side door to seat myself beside Amy. Her cheeks shine with tears, her lower lip wobbling like she isn't done crying.

'Where did you g-go?' she asks.

How am I supposed to answer that without breaking her heart? It's bad enough that I'm selling her to a glorified pimp just to give myself a new shot at life. What kind of heartless, gutless piece of work have I become?

'Ruby,' she says, then bursts into tears all over again.

I say nothing, leaning over and putting both arms around her tiny little shoulders. She trembles under my embrace, and I feel a cold stab of pity for the girl I gave birth to – for the baby I selfishly gave away because I didn't feel like there was any other choice. Is this just history repeating itself, then? How long will it be before I sell out again just to improve my own life? I couldn't possibly feel like a worse human being.

'Who are these men?' Amy asks, still sobbing.

'They're just some people who are going to take care of you,' I lie, wondering if it's too late to save her. 'They might seem scary at first, but if you trust them and do everything they say, everything is going to be okay. Just be a good girl, yeah?'

'I want my mum.'

'But you can't have her.'

'I want my dad.'

'They're not coming back, sweetheart.'

Amy whines in my arms, and my heart crumbles into a million tiny fragments. My stomach churns with anguish, and I'm only briefly pulled away from it by motion outside the car. The men have moved, shifting position just so one of them can tap on the glass and tell me it's time.

It's happening, and I've done this by thinking I could have the best of both worlds. Pulling away from Amy is the hardest thing I've ever had to do. It's not even the first time I've done it – that's how much of a piece of crap I am. Looking into her eyes now, wiping away a tear only for it to be immediately replaced, all I see is me.

Young me, wondering why my parents aren't there for me.

Slightly older me, wishing life wasn't so bad.

Current me, praying there's a way to turn all of this around.

That's when I make the decision. It's been a long time in the making, and there's no telling how it's going to pan out. But this beautiful little angel of a girl deserves far better than a rerun of the life I had. Hell, *any* kid deserves a significantly better future than that.

'I'll take care of it,' I promise her, then kiss her on the cheek.

Gathering up the envelope and the money that's falling out of it, I move for the door handle. Amy reaches out and wraps herself around my arm, begging me not to go. I tell her I'll be right back, even if it is a lie. I have to prise her fingers off me, then step out into the cold autumn air with a rush of wind assaulting me. John is there now, eyeing me sternly from a few paces away. I close the distance between us, ready to ask for one more favour.

One he won't like to give.

'I WANT TO END THE DEAL,' I say with the bravest face I can muster.

John's head darts forward and slightly crooks to one side, as if he had trouble hearing me. Ignorance is bliss, I guess. If I were in his shoes, I wouldn't want to hear something like that either. Maybe that's why I'm so sure he'll say no.

And I'm right.

'You've got to be having a laugh,' he says,

looking around at the other men, who awkwardly chortle just to please their employer. John looks around at them, his eyebrows contorted with a blend of confusion and shock, as if he can't believe what he just heard. 'Let me hear those words again, exactly as before.'

It takes everything I have to steel my nerves and obey. 'I want to end the deal.'

John punches the air and mutters something as he spins away from me, pacing in a small arc. I keep pivoting so he can't get behind me, but that doesn't stop him from trying. Truthfully, I want him right where I can see him just to be on the safe side.

As if that's going to help.

When he's done swinging about and fuming, he finally returns to me. Those deadly eyes track me once again, homing in on me as if they could kill me all by themselves. The men around us are making me nervous. I'm aware of the risks, but I also know where my heart lies.

'You realise what you're asking?' he says.

'I do.'

'Do you?'

'Yes.'

'I don't think you do. See, one major goddamn

problem is that I cannot under any circumstances give this girl back to you. The transaction is done. I've promised her to people who don't like deals being cancelled.'

We stand there in the wind. There isn't a single other sound as we all wait on his next words. All the while, my mouth is going bone dry because I have a feeling I know where this is going – what the price is for my betrayal.

'The other problem,' he goes on, starting to pace around me in circles again, like a shark intimidating its prey, 'is that now you know more than I'm willing to trust you with. No doubt you'll have gained some heat from the police by taking this girl, and there isn't a thing in this world to suggest you won't give up my name to save your own skin. If your speedy agreement to sell your own daughter isn't warning of that, I don't know what is.'

A lump forms in my throat now.

I know exactly what's coming.

John tears the envelope from my hand, smoothly checks its contents, then hands it to one of the men for safekeeping. Something tells me it's not because he's about to give Amy back. When he circles back round to stop in front of me, his cool, minty breath touching my face, I don't know where to look. I just know it shouldn't be at him.

But then it's not my choice any more. He uses a crooked finger to hook under my chin, turning my face towards his. There's murderous aggression in his eyes – the same kind of fear-inducing stare that got him so high up in his corrupt world of business. If that's not enough to strike panic into the depths of my soul, his next words certainly do the trick.

'So I can't give you the girl, and I can't let you go with the money. You know what this means, don't you? My sweet little child, this is regretfully where we part ways.'

Two of the men stride towards me. My body is drenched with cold sweat. John backs away to let the men take care of me, and I don't even question how it will be done. All I can focus on is to not scream – to not show Amy that there's anything to worry about, just to maintain the illusion of safety for one more moment.

That is my parting gift to her – to my daughter.

Only it doesn't get that far.

It's the lights that catch my attention. Soon, the attention of the men is also swept up in the chaos. The vibrant flashes of red and blue flood the sky, bleeding through the fog as they surround us. Then there are engines revving and roaring as they circle the perimeter and lock us in. It all unfolds in a heartbeat, my heart galloping at a painful pace.

That's when John turns to me, his eyes alive with ire.

'You called them!' he yells, his voice booming above even the cars.

It's hard to make out exactly what happens next because I'm numbly rooted to the ground while the men disperse, leaving only me, John, and my five-year-old on the scene. We're not all going to leave here alive, it seems.

Because John's men pull out their guns.

Chapter 28
Lizzie

Chris and I are in the car so fast I'm not even sure we locked the front door. Ed was still in the house when we left, racing out into the road and climbing into the front seats. Without so much as a single word exchanged between the two of us, we fell in perfect sync with each other – him dashing behind the wheel while I called the police to tell them what we'd learned.

It should take less than ten minutes to reach the warehouse. Five of those were spent on the phone call, but the rest are spent with raw tension tugging at my nerves. I can't stop chewing on my nails, gnawing them to the quick while Chris navigates the night-soaked roads.

'It's going to be okay,' he tells me.

'How could you possibly know that?'

'Because it is. We're always okay.'

I appreciate his optimism, but it's hard to stay relaxed when our daughter is out there being sold to... what? A sex trade? I can't even begin to imagine how I'll live with myself if the exchange is already made. And if I ever get my hands on Ruby, I'm not sure I'll be able to hold myself back. Although it seems unlikely I'd have a violent side, it must be in me.

How could it not be?

After all, I'm only human.

We arrive at the gates of the warehouse, where a scene has already formed. Thank God the police have already arrived, but damn all the citizens who have got wind of the situation and flocked to the scene. They're trying to get a glimpse of all the action. It makes moving the car impossible because the sea of curious bystanders has filled the road like ants over a picnic blanket. I'm wringing my fingers and hoping to get through this without screaming at some poor stranger. That's when Chris looks over at me.

'Get out,' he says.

'What?'

'Go by foot. Tell them who you are.'

'What will you do?'

'Find somewhere to park and catch up.'

I can't help but kiss him, already missing the real man I married so much. He's taking care of his family like he always vowed to do. No matter how hard things have been lately, he's still here. Still putting us first. That's the man I fell in love with.

'Go,' he says, this time with some urgency.

Without another word, I leap out of the car and weave between the people. There's too much nattering – talks and speculation of what's going on beyond the police barricade. Some of the theories are ridiculous, pondering the possibility of a drug deal or a murder. It doesn't even register that a murder could actually be accurate if God isn't on my side tonight.

When I reach the barricade, I shout at one of the officers and explain who I am. The young man – maybe in his mid-twenties and with all the grace of an arrogant child – looks me up and down before speaking into his radio. I can't hear what's said over all the mayhem around us, but he eventually nods and shifts the barricade aside to let me through. Before I know it, he's leading me to a small group of uniformed officers and two men in sharp suits who look at me like I'm the single most important person in the world.

As soon as they speak, I understand why they can't stop looking.

They know the severity of the situation.

FROM WHERE I'M STANDING, I can see the warehouse like an upright pillar in the night, some black cars parked close to one of the side walls, and some movement that I don't get to investigate before one of the suited men steps in the way.

'Mrs. Hughes?' he says, then doesn't wait for me to respond. 'There's something of a situation that we need to make you aware of. Can you confirm your identity as well as the fact you're the mother of Amy Hughes?'

I tremble at the mere mention of her name. Why would he ask something like that? Has something awful happened already? Is it *close* to happening? I don't notice myself answering the man because my head is swimming with emotional torture, but he moves on as soon as I give him all the information he requested.

'From what we understand,' he goes on, nodding at the uniformed men as they start to slowly disperse, 'the person who kidnapped your daughter is within sight. We're still trying to identify the men she's come to meet, but it seems they're not on the best terms.'

'What makes you say that?' I ask in a short breath.

'Body language speaks volumes, but there's also the matter of the guns.'

'What gun?' Somehow, my insides shiver.

'The men surrounding your daughter are armed. We're doing everything we can to address the situation as delicately as possible. Obviously, we'd like to avoid provoking any kind of violent outburst, but with your daughter's safety at stake, we don't want to move too fast.'

I nod, looking over his shoulder and staring as far as I can into the darkness. The figures move again, and my eyes adjust. I can see the men now, as well as Ruby in that stupid, tattered coat that makes her look every bit the whore she is. I've never felt such unbridled fury towards another person in my life. She took my daughter. She wanted to *sell* my daughter, and if Ed hadn't come by to rat on her, then who knows where Amy would be right now?

'Mrs. Hughes? Are you all right?'

I look back to the policeman, who's doing his best to show some kind of control. He's not fooling anyone – for as long as there's a gun involved and the armed police aren't on the scene, there isn't a damn thing he can do for me or my child. It makes me want to grab him by the shirt and shake him into owning the situation, but I know he's limited by procedure.

'What happens now?' I ask, my mouth all dry and my throat stony.

'Now we have to wait for...'

His voice trails off as a van stops nearby. The police have helped part the crowd to make way for them, and soon, more officers file out of the vehicle with rifles and bulletproof vests. Seeing them now makes it feel like an action film, except this is no fun. Poor, sweet little Amy is caught in the middle of this. Even if she makes it out without getting hurt, who's to say these people won't come back for her? It would take a miracle to ensure her safety, not just for tonight but for the rest of her life.

There's no telling how deep this creepy network goes.

A hand rests on my shoulder. I should jump out of my skin, but I know the feeling all too well. Chris presses his body against my back, and his arm slinks around me. While he holds me, I lean into him and no longer care about those other women. He can have a gang bang in a public bathroom for all I care, as long as he comes back to me. I know this thought will change in time, but for now, it's true because I just want one thing.

I want Amy to be safe.

'What about Ruby?' Chris asks the suited officer. 'Will she get away with this?'

'It's hard to say. As far as I can see, she's protecting your daughter.'

My head snaps around to face him. 'What?'

'That's how it looks. Amy is locked inside the car, and every time the men go for it, she starts slashing wildly at them with some sort of penknife. We can't be sure, but it looks like she's defending your daughter. Which is just as well, given the situation, but it's only a matter of time until they lose patience and shoot her.'

Chris lets go of me as I turn around to look up at him. He doesn't say a word – doesn't need to – because I know he's feeling the same mix of emotions I am. This woman we both hate, who's lied and manipulated to take Amy away from us, is now the only thing standing in the way of her ill fate. Even if she holds them off indefinitely, what then?

There's no time to answer. The armed police file onto the scene in an organised row and spill out into the gate area. The policeman excuses himself and then goes to attend a sort of huddle. Chris whispers in my ear that everything is going to be okay, but there's no way in hell he can know that. I appreciate the sentiment, but my eyes are already drifting over to the cars ahead of us, where Ruby is defending Amy with her life.

How the hell did I let this happen?

How on earth did things get so messed up?

By the time I can even start feeling sorry for myself, there's a flash coming from up ahead. It feels like the gunshot comes later. Like the crack of a whip echoing in the night. Shocked gasps explode from the crowd behind us, and all my muscles seize up at once as my brain catches up to all my other reflexes.

One of Amy's buyers has fired a gun. The armed police sweep onto the scene.

And all hell breaks loose.

. . .

More gunshots report through the night. The crowd gasps and starts to disperse, running in all directions. I, however, could never leave my daughter here. My clutch on Chris's shirt tightens. I can't look – if Amy is hurt in the middle of all that, there's no telling what I'll do. But someone fired, which means someone was probably hit.

Who was it?

Endless gunshots crack into the sky. I jump at each of them, knowing any one could destroy our lives in a heartbeat. It's hard to believe that's all it takes to turn a good life into a bad one – the simple squeeze of a trigger or the slightest miscalculation in one's aim.

There's shouting now, and I still can't look. 'Man down!' one man yells, and then two more cover it. 'Drop the weapon!' is what I hear next, nuzzling myself into Chris's chest. My husband holds me closer, assuming the role of the rock I always needed him to be.

But I can't look.

Not now.

As time goes on, I'm feeling braver. You could call it morbid curiosity because I at least want to know if the son of a bitch who wanted to buy my daughter has been gunned down. What kind of person does that make me? A villain? A monster?

A mother?

The night falls too quiet. Even the crowd has fallen to silence. The police are shuffling around us – I can hear that much – but I don't see anything until I pull away from Chris's chest, wipe a warm tear from my eye to clear my vision, then take a deep breath and dare to examine the scene with my own eyes. My heart is in my throat the whole time.

However, what I see isn't clear straight away. My horrified gaze is immediately drawn to the dead men on the ground. Two of them are motionless, like rocks and nothing more. The others are pressed onto the ground with the knees of armed police digging into their spines. Both sides are overwhelmed, which explains how *she* is getting away.

The white coat is unmistakable. She's lit up like a beacon on this cold autumn night. It's hard to make out her exact outline because the image is getting smaller as she gains more distance from the anarchy she just caused. I don't know how to feel about the idea of her escaping all of this – she might have stood her ground to save my daughter, but without her, none of this would have happened in the first place.

The mere thought of Amy is enough to make my head turn. It's as though I have a natural sense of her presence. I lose my breath when I see her. I grip Chris's arm with strength I never knew I had. She's in the custody of the armed police, escorted back to us with her innocent face soaked in tears. This will traumatise her without a doubt (just as it will all of us), but God may have taken pity on us because there are no signs of injury.

All I see – and all Chris is muttering with overwhelmed disbelief – is that our little girl has somehow escaped from the deadliest fate imaginable. She's within reach, now perking up as she spots us and breaking free from the police to dash our way. Then, I let go of my husband's arm and do the only thing I *can* do.

I run to her.

Chapter 29
Ruby

I'm glad as hell I wore my trainers tonight. My feet smack upon the tarmac as I sprint away from the scene with every last ounce of my reserve energy and then some. It's cold tonight, but I barely feel it because of the sweat. Running away from the police like this is bound to cause a little perspiration, but what really got it going was John.

I can see his face in my mind's eye now – those furious features coming to life when the cops showed up. The authorities flooded the scene and were about to come for us all. That's when John's men kept them at bay by pulling out their guns. The police stopped, coming no further than the gates while I was left to explain myself to John.

'You've got a nerve,' he spat through clenched teeth.

'I didn't call them!' I yelled over the roar of car engines and the police shouting over at us. My words were actually true, but to tell the truth, I was glad they were there. My regret for what I'd done to Amy was already pulling at my heartstrings, so imagine if I'd gone through with that dumb, selfish idea of selling my own daughter.

It was enough to make me shudder.

One of the men without the guns breezed past me and reached for my car door handle. Knowing how much trouble it would get me in, I lunged out and shoved him away. Despite the man's size, the shock had his guard down, and he stumbled to regain his balance. I expected him to turn around and smack me in the face, but instead, he only looked to his boss.

'Get the girl,' John said.

That was enough for me to snap into action.

The knife I used on Jess was still in my pocket. As the man followed orders and stomped towards me, I tore it out and slashed wildly in his direction. He leapt back, alarm widening his eyes, visible in the dark expanse of the car park thanks to the flashing police lights.

'You can't win this,' John called. 'You brought a knife to a gunfight.'

I hated how right he was. I looked around at the men surrounding me. The guns were trained on the police – who were without a doubt calling for backup – but there was no reason they couldn't be turned on me. That was when time stood still, the two alternative branches of my future appearing before me. I could lower the knife, let them take Amy, and have it over with. I'd be arrested, but at least I'd live to see morning.

Or I could stand up for what I thought was right.

I'd made a lot of mistakes in my life. Some were more disturbing than others. When I was a child, I stole a can of Coke from my grandmother when I could have just asked for it. My old man gave me a hiding and forced me to apologise. The pain from the smacked bum lasted a few minutes, but the shame was still with me to this day.

Imagine if I'd gone through with this.

It simply wasn't an option. Not any more.

Putting my back up against the car door and locking it, I dug my heels into the ground and kept a firm grip on the knife. I held it up, ready to attack anyone who dared to try taking Amy. John didn't know how to handle this – the stress of the police was stealing his attention, which was the only reason I was still alive at all.

So all we could do was wait, both equally stubborn about our needs. Meanwhile, a crowd started to form at the gates. More police cars arrived, but they all kept their distance. My hair was matted to my head with sweat for the next few minutes, and the cold was refreshing against my burning forehead. All I could do was study John's expression, praying he wouldn't give up and just have everyone murdered in a blaze of glory.

When the armed police arrived, he might as well have.

I don't know who fired the first shot, but it startled me into action. I'd been around trouble enough to know that when one bullet explodes from a gun, more usually follow. That's why my instinctive reaction was to drop the knife, open the car, and grab Amy. It all happened so fast, bullets smashing the car's glass, men shouting, my daughter bawling as I grabbed her and ran. Even as I put my hands on her and carried her out of the car, in all the chaos, I knew somehow that I would never see her again.

But if I could just do one good deed...

So I ran. Her weight in my arms was nothing. The alarming calls from the police went right over my head with the bullets. I ran to one side, far away from the gunfire, as the action unfolded. Armed officers split up, two of them coming my way to intercept me. That was good, I thought, but I didn't want to go to jail. Amy was out of the danger zone then, and that was good enough. All that was left to do was set her down and leave her there for the cops to grab her – for them to take her away and be too overwhelmed by the armed combat to open fire on me.

That was when I ran.

I moved as fast as I could, using a small outbuilding as a shield before I gained some distance. Now, here I am, disappearing into the distance while the shooting has stopped. There's no telling whether or not they'll catch me – much less whether it will be right now or somewhere down the road – but at least I can carry one positive thing with me. Just one tiny fact that will help me sleep in the years to come.

Even though I was the one who took her, at least I put an end to all of this.

Now, despite the fact I'll never see her again, Amy is safe.

And my daughter is in good hands.

I'm not stupid. Well, not completely.

I know the police are everywhere. There will be patrols, maybe even dogs, and there will sure as hell be people out looking for me. Tomorrow might be a bit easier to get around, but for tonight, I have to think about just lying low and waiting for the sun to rise.

Or rather, lying *high*.

It doesn't take too long to find an appropriate hiding spot. Lanes and back gardens are out of the question, and nothing in this world could make me sleep in a public park, but I do find the roof of a house extension that has no windows overlooking it. I can't be one hundred per cent sure if other homes have a good view of the rooftop, but I have to try my luck.

Because it's either this or a jail cell.

The roof is easy to reach, even though my hands are numb from the cold night wind. There's a low fence I'm able to stand on, which helps me crawl onto the felt. I'm slow and steady as I don't want to bang around to wake anyone up, so timing is everything. One creak makes me pause. A single scuff forces me to wait. After around five or ten minutes, I'm curled up against the wall, hiding from the world like a stray cat staying out of danger.

The problem is I'll never sleep. Not after enduring the most traumatic night of my life. Every time I close my eyes and try to steady my heartbeat, Amy's tear-stained face blinks into my imagination, like one of those persistent ads you get over online articles. I'd give anything to click it away and shut down this computer, but my mind is too busy racing.

Too many windows are open.

The wind is getting stronger. Colder. The sun will be up in a few hours, but for now, I'm stuck up here like a homeless, worthless piece of crap. It's the least I deserve, too – there's no excusing the things I've done. Promising to sell any five-year-old to a sex trade is a seriously twisted thing to do, even if I wasn't actually going to do it.

But my own daughter?

I shiver against the cold and bring my knees to my chest. Now *I* feel like the child, desperate and alone and feeling sorry for myself. A tear emerges from one eye and trickles down my numb face, but I don't bother wiping it away. I need to feel this –

to feel the sadness I brought upon myself by my own actions. Who cares if I needed money? Who gives a damn that I had a hard start in life? I have no excuse for what I've done.

Frankly, I deserve to die.

THERE'S ONLY one other person I know in Bristol, and I turn to him first thing in the morning. Some might call it a mistake, seeing as he only ever wants one thing from me. And what the hell – I'm a worthless piece of crap, aren't I? If I need to bend over just so I can have somewhere to stay, I'll do exactly that.

Gary is his name, and he's even sleazier than my older clients. Drugs and sex are his two vices, so I have the former to thank for him passing out almost immediately after. It gives me the freedom I need to pace around his small one-bedroom flat in the rougher end of St. George. Everything is brown or beige, the only exception being the whites that have been stained with cigarette smoke. That smoke has contributed to the sour odour in the air. I try not to think about it as I take a seat on his grotty old sofa and examine the goods on the cracked glass coffee table.

Three pounds and sixteen pence in change. Considering I lost my payment and my purse in last night's mayhem, this seems like a lot. Enough for a bus ride into town, maybe. Beside that, a small tub of weed and a bag of cocaine that might be worth something if I can find a buyer. It could be enough to get me out of Bristol and perhaps even give me a fresh start in a new city. Somewhere I can really make something of myself.

The alternative is suicide.

There's a knife on the table beside all those other goodies. I start gnawing on my nails, staring at my plethora of options and wondering what to do. When I'm this exhausted, cold, and dirty, it's easy to think of the coward's way out. It's always easier to give up, isn't it? To throw it all in and terminate your life just for the sake of peace? Because if I don't do that, then I've got my work cut out for me – not only would I have to find somewhere to live, work until I'm dead on my feet, and try to build a network of friends...

But I'd also have to live with what I've done.

I shiver at the thought. Amy was everything a family could have wanted. She *has* a family, and I almost took it away from her. The police will never stop hunting me for something like that, and they're very likely to find me if they somehow saw a picture of me. I'm trying to think if anyone has one, but nobody springs to mind. They don't even have my real name – just a hooker's name I created on the spot two decades ago and never thought to change.

Ruby Wishes.

Who could ever believe it was real?

Well, I've made my mind up now. As the sun creeps through the dusty old curtains that have been left open just enough to illuminate the coffee table, a glint of light bounces between the knife and the small pile of coins. It's offering me a choice for the first time in my life: should I start a new life or end the only one I have? No matter which way you look at it, there's something that's absolutely guaranteed to happen.

One way or another, Ruby Wishes dies today.

Chapter 30
Before...

SOCIAL MEDIA HAS BEEN good for one thing.

Gossip.

It was so easy to find out where my little girl ended up. A woman in Longwell Green had adopted my little girl. The woman's name was Elizabeth 'Lizzie' Dibble, and she was a pretty little thing with a bit of a librarian look to her. You'd have to dye her hair out of its natural blonde and throw a pair of glasses on her, and that would complete the aesthetic.

Finding where she lived was only slightly harder than learning who she was. I kept an eye on her from a distance, dreaming of a day when I could meet her, maybe even get to know her a little bit. She was a single woman, from the looks of things, which still surprises me to learn they let her adopt a baby by herself. I guess money could buy anything.

As I stood across the street and watched the house, a hand lay on my shoulder. I didn't jump because I knew he was there – I could always feel him when he was nearby. Maybe it's because we were good friends, or maybe he had a smell.

Could have been both.

'She named her Amy,' my friend said, resting his chin on my shoulder.

'Nice name. Not what I would have wanted, but nice.'

'Looks like she's in good hands, too.'

'It looks that way, yeah. She seems nice.'

'Hot as hell, too.'

I rolled my eyes because men always had to talk like this. Although I reckon my past experience with the opposite sex paved the way to that line of thinking. I tried not to pay it much attention, soaking in every last detail of the house my daughter was going to grow up in, hoping – praying – I would get to meet her someday.

Only if the circumstances were right.

'You'll get her back,' my friend said, soothing me.

'Why, can you perform magic?'

'No, but I wouldn't mind getting to know that woman.'

'Ugh.' I moved his hand off and started to walk away down the empty street and back into a life I despised. Just one fleeting thought of that dim future shocked me into a strange and terrifying thought. I shouldn't have asked him, but I couldn't help myself. 'Would you?'

My friend caught up to me and walked slowly by my side, his neck craned to stare down at me, his assessment of me highly suspicious. 'Would I what?'

'Would you get to know her?'

'I'm not sure what you're asking.'

'I just wondered if... maybe you could get close to her and keep watch over my baby. Perhaps one day, I might want to come back and see her. If I've got you on the inside, then it'll be a lot easier than getting past whatever poor sap she'd otherwise end up with.'

My friend laughed. 'You want me to woo a woman so you can steal her baby?'

'My baby,' I corrected him without dropping my serious expression.

'You're nuts.'

'Another reason I can't take Amy back right now.'

'You're going to work on that?'

'Sure, I'll try. So... will you?'

One last time, my friend looked over his shoulder at the house my daughter was now living in. I saw his future play out before his eyes, his lips twitching gradually from a frown into a smile. Finally, it finished converting. 'I'll give it a go, yeah. She's gorgeous and rich, so there's no reason I can't at least try. No promises though, all right?'

'All right.' I stopped and threw my arms around him, which turned into a kiss, which would at some point turn into yet another 'one-off' sexual encounter. We did that from time to time, and it was nice, but there was no romance involved. Although I must admit, tonight I really felt something for him. I needed the friend, and he was there for me even though he normally wasn't. That's why I pulled away from his lips and whispered sincerely into his ear.

'Thanks, Chris.'

Chapter 31
Lizzie

I KNOW what you're thinking. The next day, we should all be sitting around as a family and reconnecting, playing games and watching films and cherishing each other while talking about how lucky we are things didn't get even worse than they did.

Well, that's not what happens. First of all, we all took turns to shower and then slept in the same bed with Amy tucked firmly between Chris and me. Surprisingly, she fell asleep right away and started making adorable little grunting sounds as she breathed through her nose. Chris was next to follow, one of his strong arms placed over our daughter as his eyes flickered shut and his breathing became deeper, more relaxed.

I, however, didn't get to sleep until the sun rose. Motorcycles and cars passed outside, so I just listened to those like some clunky melody while trying to purge all thoughts of Ruby from my head. Even when I did finally fall asleep, my head was stuffed with nightmares about her coming back to finish what she started. This time, it would take more than a couple of warning slashes at our poor babysitter.

This time, she was out for blood.

We all wake up far into the afternoon. Chris offers to make us all a cooked breakfast, which Amy merrily agrees to as if last night's events haven't tainted her with so much as a speck of trauma. It might just be taking a while to settle in, but I let them carry on while I grab my phone off the side, change into yesterday's clothes, then head for the door.

'Where are you off to?' Chris asks.

'Just going to speak to Ed.'

'Be careful, okay?'

I nod, not worrying too much about what that old man can do to me. Ed may be a creep who used to frequent the Bristol whorehouses, but that doesn't make him dangerous. At least not on the surface.

But my curiosity is begging me to visit.

Ed lets me in with a face that suggests he was expecting me. It's like he knows I've figured something out and has no intention of putting up a fight. When he waves me through to the kitchen, I shake my head and hold my ground in the hallway.

'I'd be more comfortable right here,' I tell him. 'Besides, this won't take long.'

'Yes, I can't imagine it will. Go on, ask what you wanted to ask.'

I take a deep breath, scared to hear what I'm about to hear, then say it.

'Why didn't you tell the police what you told us?'

'Because there's more to it than what I told you.'

'You said that yesterday. But what, specifically, are you hiding?'

Ed leans with his back against the wall. When he raises a shaking hand to scratch his temple, I realise he's leaning for support. This is the end for him, and he knows it. Even though he's yet to share why. A clear of the throat starts his confession.

'Things were very different for me back then. My sweet wife was ill, and I was very lonely. It's the kind of loneliness you can't describe to another human being. People pretend they understand, but they don't. Not really.

'I didn't know how old the girls were. You have to understand that. When you're twenty-five, it's a lot easier to recognise a sixteen-year-old. When you're thirty, it's even harder. So imagine how difficult it was for a fifty-year-old soon-to-be widower.'

My lips are so dry that I have to smack my tongue against them, and I swallow an uncomfortable lump as I try to process this disturbing feeling. I can't look at Ed in the same light that I used to. Not knowing what I know now.

'So Ruby was a child,' I say with utter disdain. 'No wonder she didn't recognise you while she was here. People age, and she had a lot of customers. But you didn't get the information from her, did you?'

'No. I overheard many things. That's why I knew where they were going with Amy.'

'They almost bought her, Ed.' I'm trying (but failing) not to raise my voice. 'My daughter was almost purchased like a bloody lamp at IKEA, and you're telling me this stuff as if it doesn't mean anything – as if you made a simple mistake like eating someone else's lunch.'

'I'm sorry, I—'

'How many were there?'

'Girls?'

'Yes.' The terminology isn't lost on me. Not 'women' but 'girls'.

'Between five and ten. But more were coming.'

I scoff and turn away.

'They weren't all underage.'

'Like that makes it any better.'

'Please, Lizzie. I only told you because it might have saved your daughter.'

'Exactly. Otherwise, you would have taken this to your grave.' A nauseating feeling unsettles my stomach and makes me shake. My anger doesn't help. I've told you before that I have a violent side I'm aching to let out, and right now, I'm dying to see this man in pain. I would inflict it myself, but I've only just got Amy back, and I don't want to get locked up.

I turn back around.

'Just do one thing for me,' I say.

'Anything,' Ed says desperately.

'Tell the police everything you know.'

As he breaks down into tears, I go for the front door while digging my hand into my pocket. The phone comes out before I even reach the street, and I leave the door open so he can hear what I'm about to do. It's true that Ed saved Amy with his confession, but that doesn't mean he should go unpunished for his sins. That's why I unlock my phone.

Then make the call.

As you can imagine, the whole street comes out to view the arrest, filling up the pavements and gossiping between each other while they try to discern the cause of the commotion. I'm sitting in the window, watching and wondering what lies are currently being spread. There's always one who pretends they know the truth – they tell their friends, who tell their family, who tell *their* friends – and that's how misinformation gets around.

'Ed is a paedophile,' I mutter under my breath.

The officers are at his door for a long time. I don't know what they're talking about. Even though I crack the living room window to listen in, all I'm getting is muffled voices. After a few minutes, a strange sound whines between them. It sounds a little like an old tea kettle, but I soon realise what it is and where it's coming from.

It's Ed, crying with his confession.

I should get a kick out of this. The fact that a child molester is being arrested should put a smile on my face, but more than anything, I'm just disturbed by how long he was living this close to us. What if he looked out of his window from time to time, gazing into our garden while Amy was in her little inflatable pool? What if I asked him to watch her once or twice while I went out? 'Our children are at risk', they say on all the posters, but like death, you really don't think about how real it is until it happens to someone you know.

At least he's out of here now. I watch as the officers escort him down his garden and into the back of the police car. Ed's head is hung in shame, as it should be, and the crowd barely moves to let him through. All of their faces read pure hate and disgust, so it's quite possible they really did hear what happened.

I just feel awful about reporting it, and I don't know why.

'It's okay,' Chris says from behind me. When I turn to look at him, he offers a thin smile and sets a cup of coffee between my legs on the windowsill. 'For what it's worth, you did the right thing. One less paedophile on the street is never a bad thing.'

'I know,' I say with a sigh. 'It just feels... odd.'

'Like you can't believe it's true?'

'Exactly.'

'But he told you, using his own words.'

'Yes, it's just... you think you know a person.'

The air between us grows uncomfortable. There is more for us to talk about, but now isn't the time. Just because of how well I know Chris, I'm certain he's dying to address the problems between us rather than just sweep them under the rug. But there's a time and a place. Here and now is not it. We almost lost our daughter yesterday, and we should be over the moon.

But I'm not.

All I can think about is how close we came. All because of my poor judgement in character. I trusted Ruby around Amy, just like I trusted Ed. It's shocking how different people turn out to be after presenting themselves in a certain way. I want to avoid that in future, so I'm making a promise to myself right here and now.

From now on, I will *always* trust my gut.

Outside, the police car drives off. A line is drawn under that, so maybe we can find some peace in knowing justice will be served. Until then, there's nothing to do but cherish my family. It starts with me picking up the coffee, kissing Chris on the lips, then shuffling out of the room to find Amy, who's still drawing pictures in the living room. I think everything is okay.

For now.

The next couple of weeks are as bad as we expected. My problems with Chris have fallen by the wayside while journalists constantly harass us, and we become the talk of the town. A lot of drama happens in the Kingswood area, but nothing as big as the bust of a sex trafficking ring.

No wonder everyone is talking about it.

They've been at it for over forty years apparently, the family business being handed down to one of the men who was arrested. There's a raid on an old whorehouse in the centre of Bristol, and multiple young women are rescued from sexual slavery. It hurts to know how real it is, but they're safe now, and nothing can hurt them. Nothing except their trauma.

At least Amy is showing no signs of depression. She's her same usual, odd self, except her peculiar 'rich-folk voice' is now gone, and she's speaking incredibly loose-tongued. Apparently, a school friend of hers named Tracey-Jane has convinced her that she could grow up to be a rap star. She keeps laying the pressure on Amy to create a lyrical flow of her own, and I'm embarrassed to say she sat in her room for a full day before finally coming out to show it off. She had donned one of my old fur coats and wore sunglasses, played a rhythmic beat from my phone speaker, and hit me and Chris with her 'rap poem'.

It went something like:

My mum and my dad,
Are feeling quite bad,
'Coz I almost got taken by Ruby.
But me? I'm glad.
'Coz now I'm back,
And it ain't left me feeling moody.

The hardest part was trying not to laugh. You know what they say about turning pain into art? I think that's what she was trying to do, which was bizarrely endearing for a girl her age. I miss the rest of her rap because I fall down a rabbit hole of deep thoughts, wondering just how long it will be before she shaves one eyebrow and gets a tattoo.

At least some fun and a good, loving nature has returned to our home. It goes on like this for a couple more days, as if we actually have a shot at being a normal family again – as if we can forget everything that happened, including the one fact that keeps me up all night.

Ruby is still out there.

The men were all taken down and arrested. They're now facing trial, and I have a feeling they won't be back for a long, long time. The police have assured us that the traffickers are more focused on punishing Ruby than us – they don't seem to know our daughter's name or where she lives, but I have a personal line to call if I ever feel suspicious.

My suspicion does hit me on a Tuesday morning, just as November reaches its crescendo. It happens just as I'm heading out the door to take Amy to school – a simple buzz on my phone that I don't think too much of until I see the name on my screen. I can't even read the message yet because my heart is hammering inside my chest at the sight of her name.

Ruby.

Chapter 32
Lizzie

SHE'S ASKED to meet me, and I don't know how to feel about it. Of course, every last part of me wants to either call the police or buy a new, bigger car just so it will hurt more when I run her over. But neither is really an option, I guess.

I need to speak to you. Come to Starbucks at 9am. If you bring police I'll know.

Of course she would. The nearest Starbucks is on a retail estate. It's wide enough to see the police coming from a mile off, and there are plenty of exits for her to make an escape if she got a whiff of the authorities. To be honest, standing there in my own hallway with my car keys in hand and my daughter – *my* daughter – ready to go to school, I considered not meeting her at all. I mean... why should I? It's not like I owe her anything.

Nonetheless, I find myself standing in the Starbucks car park at exactly nine, hoping for closure. Amy is in school, and Chris is at home talking work contracts on a Zoom call with his company. I didn't call the police because there's nothing Ruby can do to me here.

Nor anything I can do to her.

It's starting to look like she's not going to turn up. A quick glance at my watch tells me it's ten minutes past, and I start to leave. It's only when I see an overdressed figure in a thick black coat with the hood up that I stop and wait to see if she comes my way.

She does, and my heart almost stops when she lowers the hood.

It's her. It's Ruby.

'I must be absolutely out of my mind by agreeing to meet you,' I say, still in half a mind to fill a pillowcase up with bars of soap just so I can beat her with it. 'You manipulated your way into our family, took advantage of my generosity, and tried to kidnap my daughter. Not even to keep her, Ruby – to *sell* her!'

'I didn't intend to sell... Look, you got every right to be angry,' she says, shaking her head with semi-sincere remorse. 'Every right. And I don't reckon any amount of apologising will make you forgive me, but I had to try. I am sorry, Lizzie. So, so sorry for what I did.'

'And all those things you told me about Chris? I'm guessing they were lies?'

Ruby's face contorts. First confusion, then softening into understanding. 'About the numbers? You know he admitted it. But there is something I need to tell you about the night he tried to seduce me. There's more—'

'One more lie out of you and I will drop-kick you off the nearest bridge.'

'It's not a lie. I just—'

'Don't test my patience.'

'Listen to me!'

Some people coming in and out of Starbucks glance over at us, but they quickly look away when I take a breath and try to calm myself. For all the good it will do. How could I possibly believe a word she has to say after everything she's done?

'I'm not proud of it,' Ruby goes on quietly. Shyly. 'But we did have sex.'

'Ruby...' My fists are clenched at my side. She's pushing her luck.

'That's not it though. There's more...'

'All right, I'm done. I don't want to hear whatever you have to say.' Just in case I'm not clear enough, I step towards her and let her see my aggressive side. Normally I would be super-nervous about something like this, but my unbridled rage is taking the reins right now. 'Let me spell this out for you so you understand me loud and clear. I don't want you to ever contact me again. I don't want to hear your name again, and I certainly don't want to see it light up my phone screen. You'll never see Amy again – not even come close – so the best thing you can do for everyone right now is go find a quiet place to die. You hear me?'

Ruby bursts into tears, but she doesn't move an inch. Apparently, she's more upset by my hatred than scared by my threats. I don't blame her either – even at my most angry, I'm hardly intimidating. But still, there's a sincerity in her now that I haven't seen before. Like her entire mission or purpose has been stripped from her, and now she's nothing but vulnerable.

Just like my daughter was.

'I just want to tell you,' she begins, 'because you deserve to know.'

'What could you possibly have to say that I would believe?'

'But you *have* to believe me. It's the truth.'

'Then you can prove it to me or get the hell away from me.' I jab a finger into her ribs so hard that even the cushion of her padded coat isn't enough to protect her. She steps back, her open mouth a wide hole of surprise. 'Get out of here right now, Ruby. I'm going to call the police in thirty seconds, and that's final.'

'Please, just—'

'Thirty.'

'Wait.'

'Twenty-nine.'

The counting continues in my head while she studies me, probably to see if I'm serious. I am – *deadly* serious – and she seems to recognise that after looking me up and down a couple of times. Then, when I truly don't expect her to do so, she turns around and runs away from me. Behind Starbucks and out of sight. Out of my life. Hopefully forever.

But what has hope ever done for me?

. . .

I DON'T TELL Chris what happened with Ruby, and I don't know why. A part of me is inclined to believe what she said – that they did have sex and that she only told half the story before so she could protect her interest in... well, kidnapping Amy. Maybe a day will come when I find the right words to ask him about it.

For now, I'll believe what's easiest for me.

The police call me five days later with some news I never expected. Ruby was found on a street in the city centre, wrapped up in a sleeping bag outside a shop with a needle in her arm. She was dead when they found her, and there's no way to ever find out if she did it to herself on purpose. I feel a bizarre tug from two opposing emotions: guilt and relief.

Was this my fault?

Look, I'm a pretty calm person by nature. I like to think recent events have expressed that I'm relaxed, kind, and compassionate. So when I told Ruby to go and die, it was only because she found my weak spot, then proceeded to press and press. Now that she's actually gone ahead and done it, what am I supposed to feel?

There's a weird brush of sadness when I hang up the phone. Ruby didn't know anyone – there's nobody to take care of her funeral arrangements or even attend. Is this my responsibility? Should I be telling Amy the truth about her origins? Is she entitled to a shot at saying goodbye to her birth mother in a formal ceremony?

No, she's better off not knowing.

But there is one other thing.

Two days ago, there was a text from Ruby. I swiped it from my notification bar when it came in because I wasn't sure how to deal with my emotions upon seeing her name. Now that she's officially a thing of the past, I spend a few minutes staring blankly out the window and trying to process what happened to her.

Only after a great deal of time am I able to actually read it.

I instantly regret doing so.

It reads:

I wasn't lying when I said about Chris. We go a lot further back than we led you to believe. He's been my friend for twenty years. We used to drink together, sometimes even do drugs. When I gave Amy away, we agreed he would make a move on you, get close to you so I could take her back someday. But when the time actually came, I think he truly fell in love with you. That's why he kept trying to push me away. He didn't want me to destroy his perfect little family. And by the way, we DID have sex. It wasn't the first time, either. I've attached some photos as proof and hope that maybe someday you can forgive me for the many things I did to you. It might not mean much, but I truly am sorry.

Kelly Welsh
AKA Ruby Wishes

My hands are trembling so hard it's like they have their own vibrate function. Heat snakes up my neck, and before long, I'm gritting my teeth. After reading the words, I really don't want any of them to be true. But when I scan through the pictures, there's no denying it.

They're pixelated as if taken from an older phone, but they're clear enough to see younger versions of Ruby and Chris... arm in arm... mouth to mouth... partying, having fun, doing all the things he and I should have been doing together. There are screenshots of text messages between the two, him begging her not to tell me the truth. There's an old mugshot, taken after being arrested for stealing a hi-fi system from Woolworths back in the day, or so the caption says. It's essentially a whole file on a man I thought I knew.

I feel sick to my stomach. Nothing could have prepared me for any of this.

Much less for what's going to happen next.

THERE's no clear way to explain how I'm feeling.

I have an endless supply of rage provided by my daughter's real mother. Now that she's gone, there's nobody to take it out on. I could ask Chris for the truth about what happened all those years ago, but there's not a doubt in my mind that his answer would be as fake as the past few years have been. Now that Ruby is dead and the evidence of his guilt is sitting on my phone, I'm left with a problem I don't know how to handle.

All I can do is trust my gut.

I find him and Amy in the living room. Amy is sitting on his lap and watching *Moana* for the millionth time, her 50 Cent beanie pulled down to just above her eyebrows. She looks vegetative, as does Chris, who has fallen asleep with his arms by his sides.

This is how I'll do it.

First, I wave Amy to my place in the doorway. She slides off her father without question, then makes her way towards me. Chris doesn't stir. I lower myself to one knee and tell her I'll be buying her a big present of her choosing, as long as she goes upstairs for a few minutes. I'm lying, of course, because who knows what life will be like minutes from now?

Amy nods excitedly and pounds up the stairs. I wince because it might wake Chris, but it doesn't. His head is tilted back, a small slug of saliva creeping from the corner of his mouth. For the first time in my entire life, I hate him with every fibre of my being. It's not just the trouble with those ladies' numbers that bugs me now but the fact he's been lying to me since the day we met – that he's slept with Ruby and lied to my face about it.

That he's dangerous, and I can no longer trust him around our daughter.

All those rushes of disdain I had for Ruby I now feel for him. All the anger I was saving for her now belongs to him. All the aggression... and the violence.

I'm barely in control when my hand reaches for the paperweight on the bureau, my fingers coiling around it like a snake seizing its prey. I feel light-headed as vengeance and weeks of anger make my blood boil. It doesn't even feel like my own body making the motion – the single swipe that ends my husband's life within a few short seconds. But the horrific flood of guilt and self-hatred that drowns me in tears as soon as it's done?

That will be mine forever.

For other books by AJ Carter, visit:

www.ajcarterbooks.com/books

About the Author

AJ Carter is a psychological thriller author from Bristol, England. His first book, *The Family Secret*, is praised by critics around the world, and he continues to regularly deliver suspenseful novels you can't put down.

Sign up to his mailing list today and be the first to hear about upcoming releases and hot new deals for existing books. You'll also receive a FREE digital copy of *The Couple Downstairs* – an unputdownable domestic thriller you won't find anywhere else in the world.

www.ajcarterbooks.com/subscribe

Printed in Great Britain
by Amazon

38910083R00189